BETRAYAL

by
Ching-Hsi Perng and Fang Chen
English Translation by Ching-Hsi Perng

STUDENT BOOK CO., LTD.

BETRAYAL

by Ching-Hsi Perng and Fang Chen

English Translation by Ching-Hsi Perng

Copyright © 2013 Ching-Hsi Perng and Fang Chen
cueariel@gmail.com

No.11, Lane 75, Sec. 1, He-Ping E. Rd., Taipei, Taiwan
http://www.studentbook.com.tw
email: student.book@msa.hinet.net

ISBN 978-957-15-1589-2

[Don't] waste [your time] living someone else's life. Don't be
trapped by dogma . . . . Don't let the noise of others'
opinions drown out your own inner voice.

Steve Jobs (1955-2011)

What we do know is that Shakespeare constantly refashioned
the works of others and that he expected in turn that his own
works would be similarly refashioned.

Stephen Greenblatt

. . . of course, the culture writes us first, and then we write
our stories.

Charles Mee

Preface: The *Cardenio* Project

Stephen Greenblatt
Harvard University

Shakespeare's imagination worked by restless appropriation, adaptation, and transformation: he was certainly capable of making stories up on his own, as in *A Midsummer Night's Dream*, but he clearly preferred picking something up ready-made and moving it into his own sphere, as if the phenomenon of mobility itself gave him pleasure. And he never hinted that the mobility would now have to stop: on the contrary, he seems to have deliberately opened his plays to the possibility of ceaseless change. The multiple texts in which several of his major plays exist – including, among others, *Romeo and Juliet, Hamlet, Othello,* and *King Lear* – suggest that Shakespeare and his company felt comfortable making numerous cuts, additions, and other changes perhaps linked to particular performances, playspaces, and time constraints. This comfort-level, registered intimately in the remarkable openness of the plays to reinterpretation and refashioning, has contributed to the startling longevity of Shakespeare's achievement: the plays lend themselves to metamorphosis.

But the question remains: how can one do justice to theatrical mobility, that is, how can one get sufficiently close and inward with its processes in order to study it and to understand it? Several years ago I felt I had at least glimpsed a possibility when I first encountered the brilliant work of a contemporary American playwright, Charles Mee. Mee is a cunning recycler who is particularly gifted at registering the original charge of the material he has lifted while moving that material in new and unexpected directions. I had been especially dazzled by a play, *Big Love,* which Mee largely created out of the odd, surviving fragments of lost Greek plays and had been greatly impressed as well by his many other plays, which he generally posts, without copyright protection, on a website that encourages others to feel free to use them in an ongoing process of appropriation and transformation.

I contacted Mee and told him that I would like the opportunity to watch the creation of one of his plays, from its first inception to its actual production. Throughout my career, I explained, I had been studying the creative mobilization of cultural materials in Shakespeare, but it was always at a 400-year distance. I wanted to be able to be close enough to track and understand every move, and I could only hope to do that with a living playwright, someone to whom I could ask questions and from whom I could get direct answers. I added that I had received a generous grant from the Mellon Foundation that would enable me to pay – handsomely, by the standards of a working playwright -- for this privilege.

Mee declined. He was not interested in money, he said, and he did not particularly like being watched. But, he added, if I could come up with an idea for a play, he would consider writing something with me. For a Shakespearean, the choice was a fairly obvious one: I proposed that we write a modern version of Shakespeare's lost play, *Cardenio*. This was a play written in collaboration with his younger colleague, John Fletcher, whom Shakespeare near the end of his career seems to have chosen as his successor. Two of their collaborations – *Henry VIII (All Is True)* and *The Two Noble Kinsmen* – survive, but *Cardenio*, performed on several documented occasions in 1613 and registered for print in mid-century, does not. The reason for its disappearance is unclear but entirely unsurprising: only a fraction of sixteenth and seventeenth century plays were preserved.

Shakespeare and Fletcher evidently took their plot from the story of Cardenio as it is episodically recounted in Part One of Cervantes' *Don Quixote* (1605). When we set out to devise a modern version of *Cardenio*, Charles Mee and I started in the obvious place, with the Cardenio story, but we immediately ran into a problem: the story seemed relatively difficult to set in motion. The difficulty lay not in its themes of betrayal and madness. Rather, it lay in the motivating premise of an immensely powerful social hierarchy – something far more compelling than wealth alone -- that allows the plot to unfold.

Mee and I could have found some contemporary equivalent to the hierarchical social code of the Renaissance – in the army perhaps, or in certain extreme business or academic communities. But the task felt artificial and labored, and successful aesthetic mobility thrives on ease or at least on the illusion of ease. Where something immediately clicked for us was not in the principal Cardenio story but rather in the distorted mirror-image of that story that a priest in Cervantes' novel reads to Cardenio at an inn.

The priest's story centers on a young man, Anselmo, whose irrational anxiety about his wife's fidelity leads him to insist that his best friend Lothario attempt to seduce her. The story has a predictably disastrous outcome, but we chose to give it an ending suitable for a comedy.

The version of *Cardenio* that Charles Mee and I wrote and that was performed at the American Repertory Theatre in Cambridge in 2008 incorporates a series of characteristic Shakespearean motifs. It is a celebration of the impulses of the heart and the willingness to gamble on love. And the plot as a whole drives, as Shakespearean comedy so often does, through confusion to clarification and forgiveness.

The project was an experiment that enabled me to explore the interplay of freedom and constraint in the practice of cultural mobility of which Shakespeare was the great master. I decided to explore it further with an additional experiment. Making contact with theater companies in different parts of the world, I invited them to take the same materials, now including the play Mee and I had written, and to rework them into a form that is appropriate for their particular culture.

I have been privileged to witness an array of these adaptations: in India, Japan, Turkey, Spain, Brazil, South Africa, Serbia, Croatia, Egypt, and now, as the final and climactic instance, Taiwan. The scripts, production details, and performance videos have been posted on a website. The productions I have seen have confirmed in remarkable detail the blend of contingency, license, and constraint that characterized my own personal experience of cultural mobility. None of the adaptations closely resembles the other, and none replicates our own play, though all clearly derive from the narrative materials we had provided and all are, in significant ways, versions of the Cardenio story. Taken together, they reveal the extraordinary force of diverse national theatrical traditions. They provide powerful clues to the ways in which the human imagination in a particular place and time is shaped by its distinct history and shapes in turn whatever it takes within its creative grasp.

Foreword

Betrayal is inspired by Stephen Greenblatt and Charles Mee's contemporary drama *Cardenio*, which in turn derives from Shakespeare's "lost play" *Cardenio* and an episode in Cervantes's *Don Quijote de la Mancha*. Focusing on this play's transmutations, Professor Greenblatt of Harvard University, under the aegis of The Andrew W. Mellon Foundation, started "The *Cardenio* Project: An Experiment in Cultural Mobility" (2003-). (For details see http://www.fas.harvard.edu/~cardenio/index.html.) Thus Cardenio, whom Don Quijote chanced to meet, has now been turned into the protagonist in many a cross-cultural adaptation.

There's only one stipulation for the adaptations taking part in the experiment: they should not be mere "translations" of the "original"; they should "betray" it! Such appropriations are bound to take into consideration local cultures. In other words, this kind of betrayal highlights the adaptors' truthfulness to their vision of their own culture. Betrayal thus becomes a different form of loyalty.

Betrayal, the twelfth play to join in this experiment of cultural mobility, is concerned about what "betrayal" means in the contexts of traditional Chinese culture and modern time. It is based on the belief that the individual's search for an ideal love should be given a chance and treated with magnanimity and understanding even in the patriarchal society. Betrayal is no betrayal, when it is merely a harmless form of truthfulness to one's ideal. In this play, the protagonists' rebellious acts bode well for the country and the houses involved, for the firstborn yields his primogenital rights in favor of his younger brother, a more qualified future leader of the country. Moreover, love triumphs over fate, thus putting an end to bloody retaliations.

At first glance, the present play may seem a far cry from Greenblatt and Charles Mee's American *Cardenio* and hence smacks of infidelity. But one must not forget their version is not any more similar to its sources. Thus infidelity becomes a form of fidelity. As to the echoes and dialogues between these two plays, we leave it to the discerning reader familiar with *Cardenio* to detect them.

We are extremely grateful to Professor Greenblatt whose preface graces this book; to The Mellon Foundation for its generous support; to Professor Daniel S. P. Yang, Professor Hui-Fen Liu, and Professor Bao-Chun Lee, for their valuable suggestions at various stages of the writing of this play; to Mr. Yi-Chien Chou for allowing us to print the musical scores he wrote for the play; and to Ms. Hui-Ju Chen for the beautiful cover design.

Translator's Note:

Again, it is with great pleasure and most sincere gratitude
that I record here my indebtedness to
two admirable friends—
Tom Sellari, Poet, Shakespearean Scholar, and Professor
at National Chengchi University, Taiwan,
and
Joseph Graves, accomplished Actor, Director, Playwright,
and
Artistic Director of Peking University's
Institute of Theater and Film.
They read an earlier version of the translation
with loving care and critical acumen
and offered a wealth of useful suggestions for
improvement,
most of which have been incorporated here.
Any infelicities that remain are of course
solely my responsibility.

Table of Contents

BETRAYAL

By Ching-Hsi Perng and Fang Chen
(Inspired by Stephen Greenblatt and Charles Mee's *CARDENIO*)
English translation by Ching-Hsi Perng

List of Characters

YIXIANG	Princess of the former Empire of Zhuque (i.e., "Rose Finch"); beloved disciple of Old Man
PRINCESS	Yulan, Princess of the Empire of Xuanwu (i.e., "Black Tortoise")
XINGYUAN	The young master, elder son of the Prince of Jingnan
SHIYUAN	The younger master, second son of the Prince of Jingnan
PRINCE OF JINGNAN	Kinsman of the Emperor of Canglong (i.e., "Green Dragon"), a general of illustrious military achievements
OLD MAN	Yixiang's master, one-time Chief Commander of Zhuque's imperial guards
NANNY QIAO	Old nursemaid in service of the royal house of Jingnan
HUAMEI	Princess Yulan's personal lady-in-waiting
GENERAL KE	Commander of Guards of the Jingnan court

Several Maidservants

Several Ladies-in-Waiting

Several Guards

List of Scenes

Prologue

The palace of PRINCE OF JINGNAN, *of the Empire of Canglong,
decorated with lanterns and colored ribbons, is awash with joy.
Maidservants are busy decorating the Flowered Hall.*

[Chorus, *offstage*]:
> **The sky is cloudless, spring is here;**
> **The day felicitous, the flowers bloom.**
> **A blessed marriage preordained**
> **Begins with a journey long and rough.**
> **Emblazoned Xuanwu banners flapping,**
> **The princess' retinue'll to Canglong march.**

Scene 1: Marriage Declined

The Flowered Hall of the palace of PRINCE OF JINGNAN.

[Maidservants *sing in unison*]

> **Ready—ready, ready to bid welcome to the bride;**
> **O joy, O joy, O joy has come a-calling!**
> **Two royal houses joined in jubilance—**
> **Indeed a perfect match in heaven made.** (*reprise*)

MAIDSERVANT 1: (*cleaning a table*) . . . they should've started out long ago.

MAIDSERVANT 2: (*moving a chair*) Should've arrived at the border by now, if you count the days.

MAIDSERVANT 3: (*hanging a painting, she turns her head*) Yeah. I heard from Nanny Qiao that Xuanwu has sent a huge escort to attend the princess. Three or four hundred at least!

MAIDSERVANT 1: Emperor Xuanwu, they say, is so reluctant to part with his beloved daughter, he's not only designated troops of Nu-Star Banner and Xu-Star Banner as escorts, but those of Dou-Star Banner and Niu-Star Banner to lead the way!

MAIDSERVANT 3: Well, then, do we not have to do likewise and send out all our seven star-banners?

MAIDSERVANT 1: Indeed! Troops of Jiao-Star and Kang-Star are already at the border, in anticipation of the bridal sedan chair. And the troops of Di-Star and Fang-Star departed two days ago. Our young master has received command to welcome the princess in person at Mulberry Field with the troop of Xin-Star. Today, the fifteenth, is a lucky day to set out on a journey.

MAIDSERVANT 2: Looks like His Majesty makes much of our young master.

MAIDSERVANT 1: That's for sure. Not only is our young master handsome and dignified, he is also skilled in literary as well as martial arts. . . . Who else deserves such favor?

MAIDSERVANT 2: Well, then, is this Princess Yulan of Xuanwu beautiful, do you know? Is she tender-hearted? Are they a perfect match?

MAIDSERVANT 3: (*shaking her head*) I don't know.

MAIDSERVANT 1: (*shaking her head*) I don't, either.

NANNY QIAO *enters, on a walking stick.*

NANNY QIAO: You silly girls! When two emperors strike an alliance by way of marriage, who cares about looks? Be they green beans or sesame, the most important thing is they match in social rank! Get on with your work, and stop chattering!

MAIDSERVANT 1 *shrugs while* MAIDSERVANT 2 *makes a face; they glance at each other and get on with their work.*

MAIDSERVANT 3: (*stepping forward*) Hi, Nanny Qiao! (*Having sat* QIAO *down, she massages her back ingratiatingly*) Take a rest, Nanny, there's no hurry. Now look, isn't everything in perfect order? What's there to worry about?

NANNY QIAO: (*looking around and pointing here and there*) Well, well, well. You can't be too fussy about wedding preparations. If the scrolls on the wall do not hang straight, it will bring ill luck. . . . If one "double blessings" is missing from the window, that means "blessings will be incomplete." . . . Too much water in the vase, and the flowers turn yellow; too little, and they wither. Move things around gingerly; shut the windows when the wind blows. And here . . . ayyo! . . . hurry up, there are many other things to look after! . . .

MAIDSERVANTS 1, 2, *and* 3 *get busy as they follow the instructions of* NANNY QIAO, *who exits as she gives order.*

Shadows appear on stage. GUARDS *enter in groups, singing while searching.*

Guards (*sing in unison*):

Look, look, look, look everywhere,

Search, search, search, search carefully.

Aiya!—

How unexpected! Who could've foretold

That a perfect match should change so suddenly,

like dark clouds appearing on a sunny day;

A perfect match should change so suddenly, like

dark clouds appearing on a sunny day.

NANNY QIAO: (*stepping forward, hails the commander of guards*)
Hey, hey, General Ke . . .

GENERAL KE *pays no attention, as if he had not heard
her.*

NANNY QIAO: I say, General Ke . . .

GENERAL KE: Oh, it's you, Nanny Qiao!

NANNY QIAO: What's all this hurry-scurry? What are you looking
for? Aren't you supposed to be on your way already? It
would be terrible to have missed the auspicious hour!

GENERAL KE: (*looking around, then in a low voice*) Well, I
suppose it's all right to tell you, but you must keep quiet.

NANNY QIAO: What exactly is the matter?

GENERAL KE: The Xin-Star Banner troop has been waiting for
quite a while, and it's long past the appointed time, and yet
the young master is nowhere to be found.

NANNY QIAO: What? The young master has disappeared?

GENERAL KE: Not so loud, please!

NANNY QIAO: Where did he go? Why didn't he tell me? I'm his nurse! Since he lost his mother, he has been trusted to my care. Whatever he thinks or does, there's nothing that I'm not privy to. Perhaps he's practicing swordsmanship in the Assembly Hall of the Virtuous and forgot the time? Go there and maybe you can find him. . . .

GENERAL KE: (*interrupting her*) Dear Nanny, we've searched everywhere in the palace. The young master—it seems he's run away.

NANNY QIAO: Nonsense! This marriage is going to link the two empires. Already the heir apparent of Jingnan and adopted son of the emperor of Canglong, he'll soon be the son-in-law of the emperor of Xuanwu—with endless glories and riches awaiting him. Why would he run away?

GENERAL KE: But the young master has left a letter, which says clearly—

(*Voice offstage*) . . . Incompetent though I am, I have been blessed with ancestral protection and become the lineal heir. Furthermore, by boundless imperial favor I have been given a golden match, most noble in rank and splendid in fame, though not my desert. As the royal favors Your Grace and

His Majesty have showered on me I can never requite, so by reason I should strive to acquit myself with the utmost thoughtfulness in discharging my filial duty. And yet, life is short and our days fleeting. In this life what should one look for? Nothing but a person of kindred spirit. Slow-witted though I am, I would hope to solve this life's puzzle. Thus am I emboldened to beg on my knees that you retract your published command. . . .

NANNY QIAO: Ah? What? I know not a word of all this gabbling and jabbering of genteel language.

GENERAL KE: Oh, well, Nanny Qiao! (*mimes to the tune of* "San Qiang") Thus and thus—isn't it an open (*lowering his voice*) rejection of the marriage?

NANNY QIAO: What are you talking about? Rejection of the marriage? Where's the letter? I'll go see it.

GENERAL KE: My dear nanny, what's there for you to see, if you can't read?

NANNY QIAO: Humph! Although I can't read, I can verify the handwriting!

GENERAL KE: Yes, yes, of course. His Grace had it in his hand when he called in the younger master.

NANNY QIAO: Why would he call in the younger master?

GENERAL KE: Ai! If the young master should oppose the

command and decline the marriage, what consequence . . .

NANNY QIAO: What's to be done?

GENERAL KE: So, His Grace has commanded that I go search for the young master immediately. Meanwhile, as an expediency, we can only send the younger master to take his place and stall for time. (*becoming aware of the time of day*) Aiya, Nanny Qiao, it's getting late, and I have business to take care of. Excuse me. (*hurries off*)

NANNY QIAO: (*mumbling to herself*) The young master declines the marriage in such a stealthy way? Running away? I can't believe it! Pulling the wool over my eyes, eh? I'll get to the bottom of it. (*Exit.*)

Light dims.

Scene 2: The Encounter

The bottom of Peach Blossom Valley, with a labyrinth outside of it. Section A: a house; Section B: a pavilion; Section C: a rocky den.

> *(Section A)*
> *A soft, clear female singing voice, accompanied by a zither, is heard:*

> **Green mossy paths are wet with rain,**
> **Flowering arbors drenched by chilly dew . . . .**

XINGYUAN, *lying on a stone slab, is slowly waking up. He looks around confusedly, then walks outside and discovers chirping birds and fragrant blossoms—*

The singing continues:
> **Most beauties are ill-starred,**
> **They wander aimlessly in life . . .**

XINGYUAN: Where am I? How did I get here? This song . . .

He walks in the direction of the song, only to lose his way.

What? The bridge, the creek, these Hushan pebbles, the peony railing, the peach blossom pavilion . . . I'm not dreaming, am I?

XINGYUAN *walks into Section B as light fades out on Section A.*

Light fades in on Section B, discovering YIXIANG *singing while playing a zither.*

YIXIANG: (*continues singing*)

> **What's past 'tis useless to recall,**
>
> **Alas! I'll leave it to the eastward wind . . .**

XINGYUAN: (*aside*) Ya! Who's this . . . that sings so mournfully?

He steps forward and peeks through flower clumps.

YIXIANG: (*continues singing*)

> **The tune of "Playful Plum Blossom,"**
>
> **Though wordless, says it all for me.**

XINGYUAN: (*aside*) This young lady—

(*sings an aside*)

> **So gentle, graceful, far beyond all words;**
>
> **Like a chrysanthemum, she wears no powder and**
> **no paint.**
>
> **Did she light from the palace of the moon?**
>
> **Her charm outdoes begonias in bloom.**

(*speaks an aside*) Such a young beauty, how could she . . . ?

YIXIANG: (*suddenly aware of being watched*) Who's there?

XINGYUAN: (*walking out of the clumps, salutes*) For the impolite intrusion, I crave your forgiveness.

YIXIANG: (*returns the salute*): Well, so it's the heir apparent of Jingnan!

XINGYUAN: (*surprised*) Who are you, lady? How do you know me?

YIXIANG: This is a quiet, secluded place with hardly any visitors. When my master took you home last night, he explained everything to me.

XINGYUAN: (*recalling*) Last night . . . all I remember was . . . I was reading *The Classic of Mountains and Seas*, where it says . . . in a remote, arid place there stands Mount Hexu, from which the Sun and the Moon come out . . . . (*suspecting*) Ah? Was I hit by a "soul-snatching perfume"?

YIXIANG *smiles without answering.*

XINGYUAN: (*looking around*) What's this place?

YIXIANG: Peach Blossom Valley. (*pauses*) My master says you're invited to be his guest here for some days. He will take you back on the fifteenth of next month.

XINGYUAN: (*suddenly alarmed*) What day's today?

YIXIANG: The seventeenth of the third month.

XINGYUAN: Oh, no! I have to be back immediately. Who's your master?

YIXIANG: He told me to tell no one.

XINGYUAN: I have to see him on urgent business. Would you
please announce me?

YIXIANG: My master went out early in the morning.

XINGYUAN: Why would he keep me here?

YIXIANG: Well, I don't really know.

XINGYUAN: What if I don't want to stay?

YIXIANG: I'm afraid you have no choice.

XINGYUAN: Ha, ha! I've trained in martial arts since childhood, and
am skilled in Canglong Fencing Methods handed down
from old. This tiny Peach Blossom Valley, how can it
detain me? (*pauses*) Now you will have to excuse me.

Turning around, he starts to run. YIXIANG *smiles in silence.*
XINGYUAN *goes along the winding paths, fighting back
miracle warriors with his Canglong fencing skill, but
eventually comes back to where he started.*

XINGYUAN: Ya? How can I still be at the Pavilion?

*He tries two more times, confronting different miracle
warriors, and still ends up where he started.*

XINGYUAN: (*catching* YIXIANG *smiling*) Why are you smiling? Is
this . . . is this a labyrinth?

YIXIANG: (*nodding*) Yes.

XINGYUAN: Aha! What a fine miraculous labyrinth!

He thinks for a moment, then suddenly points his sword at YIXIANG.

XINGYUAN: Well, then, lady, I have to trouble you to lead the way out.

YIXIANG *jerks her sleeve and out come peach blossom petals; immediately* XINGYUAN *drops his sword and falls feebly on a stone chair.*

XINGYUAN: (*shocked*) Ah! What's this? Why do I suddenly feel so weak?

YIXIANG: Well, it's nothing but the "Wispy Fragrance" that I concocted. Its effect doesn't last long, just four hours. As long as you do not exert yourself, you'll be all right. (*pauses*) Your highness, now that you're here, you might as well make yourself comfortable. Don't let your thoughts run wild.

Casually she plucks some notes on the zither.

XINGYUAN: Well! (*helpless*) I've been too rude, and have offended you.

YIXIANG: (*smiles brightly*) Never mind. (*pauses*) You must be hungry by now. Wait here and I'll be right back. (*exit*)

XINGYUAN: Ya! (*sings*)

> **This young lady, mystifying yet considerate,**
> **An orchid seems that stands alone in valley deep.**
> **Her inscrutable master, what means he by this?**
> **Uneasy sitting or standing, I keep wandering in**
> **mind.**
> **Concerned am I about the royal marriage, but**
> **There is no way to get out of this plight.**

Re-enter YIXIANG, *with a tray.*

YIXIANG: Sir, take this while it's hot.

XINGYUAN: Well. . . (*a bit hesitant*)

YIXIANG: Don't worry, it's not poisoned. You are a distinguished
guest here, so we will show you our utmost hospitality.

XINGYUAN: All right. Thank you! (*starts to take in mouthfuls*) Ah!
So refreshingly aromatic! What are these?

YIXIANG: (*smilingly*) They are our homemade peach blossom cakes
and peach rolls, and this is home-brewed liquor made from
peaches picked in spring, plus some dried peach and
plum . . . .

XINGYUAN: (*quaffs the liquor*) Such bouquet! It tastes so pure,
refreshing, and natural. How is it made?

YIXIANG: The liquor? (*slightly proud*) It's done in no ordinary way, but according to a yeast-infusion distilling method that my master invented. There are twelve steps, and the powdered ingredients have to be put in bags made of unglued raw silk, and nine times immersed in cold water in a tightly sealed jar. The ingredients alone number a dozen items. The process is too complicated and trivial to be of interest to a person of your high rank, I suppose?

XINGYUAN: Not at all (*takes another swig*) . . . er, lady, how should I call you?

YIXIANG: Yixiang is my name.

XINGYUAN: Lady Yixiang, I've never tasted such delicious wine in my royal house. (*salutes with cupped hands*) Do instruct me.

YIXIANG: Well, Your Highness—

(*sings*)

> **Plump grains from golden ears of rice**
> **Are buried at the bottom of a jar to serve as yeast.**
> **On tulip leaves are spread crape myrtles;**
> **Proud suns shall bake white pears.**
> **Then peach stamens taken on the vernal equinox,**
> **To mix with apricot root finely ground. . . .**

XINGYUAN: That sounds laborious!

YIXIANG: (*continues singing*)

> **On Day of Grain Rain, heat it with boiling water.**

And don't forget some music to amuse the plants.

XINGYUAN: Oh? You have to play the zither to them? If so, where can you plant them?

YIXIANG: (*continues singing*)

By the natural den so dark and deep,
A sep'rate zither table have we set.

XINGYUAN: (*curious*) A separate zither table? May I see?

YIXIANG: (*nodding*): Yes, please. (*they stand up*)

(*she continues singing*)

To decorate the scene with flora day and night,
Layers of lively green have been arranged.

They take the winding path to Section C.

YIXIANG: (*speaks as she leads the way*) Every plant, in fact, has its own favorite music, just like every human being. For example, peaches and apricots are partial to the tune "Chanting in Spring Morning," Sichuan lovage likes "Temple Incantation," the herbaceous peony enjoys "Flowing Water," the balloon flower adores "Guangling San" . . .

XINGYUAN: (*amazed*) How do you know so much?

YIXIANG: I learned it from my master.

XINGYUAN: Oh? What about your parents?

YIXIANG: (*ready to cry any moment, she stops*) Well, . . . (*walks on* *again*)

XINGYUAN: What's the matter? Why did you come to this Peach
　　　Blossom Valley?

YIXIANG: (*shaking her head*) I don't know. Ever since I can
　　　remember, I've been living with my master. He is very kind
　　　to me, but he's never mentioned my parentage. He just says
　　　I'm an orphan. . . . (*unable to hold back her tears, she
　　　wipes them*)

XINGYUAN: I'm sorry to have made you sad.

YIXIANG: It's nothing. Fates differ from person to person.
　　　(*pretending cheerfulness*) At least I have my master.
　　　(*she comes to a halt*) There, here we are.

Section C lights up.

XINGYUAN: (*changing the topic on purpose*) What a huge rock den!

YIXIANG: Is it? We do our best to make the plants feel comfortable,
　　　so that they will grow better. (*pointing to a tree*) Take for
　　　instance this peach tree. It is nicknamed "Spring Bud." It
　　　starts to bear fruit in late March; if you play the tune of
　　　"Chanting on Spring Morning" at that time, its fruit will be
　　　especially plump and smooth; a tad sour in sweetness and
　　　richly aromatic—a unique flavor.

XINGYUAN: Shame on me! I just keep sampling the delicacies,
　　　without even thinking about how they were made. . . .

(*pointing at another plant*) And what is that?

YIXIANG: Oh, that's raspberry. It'll take two more months to bear fruit. When its fruit is steamed and dried, we keep it in powder form. There's some raspberry powder in the cake you just ate.

XINGYUAN: Ah, no wonder it had a special flavor, which lingers even now.

(*looking around*) So many plants—do you take care of them all by yourself?

YIXIANG: My master used to help. These days he's been too busy, so there's only me.

XINGYUAN: Well, then, it is a very hard job!

YIXIANG: Well, then, in this world there are many very hard jobs.

XINGYUAN: You mean . . .

YIXIANG: I mean—

(*sings*)

Haven't you heard,

The God of Medicine would taste all kinds of herbs,

And Goddess Nu Wa fired stones to patch the sky?

Haven't you heard,

Kua Fu raced all the way to Lingbao in chase of the sun,

And Jingwei carried sprigs to fill the vastness of the sea?

They start to sing a duet.

XINGYUAN: What exertion! How hazardous!

You've got to get through by yourself.

YIXIANG: Did they not know the dangers of the path they
took?

Easy or not? On a turn of thought it all depends.

XINGYUAN: To drift with the tide

YIXIANG: Will never do;

XINGYUAN: I'll search my soul

YIXIANG: And fulfill my will.

XINGYUAN: Love supreme admits no rue

YIXIANG: Nor any grudge;

XINGYUAN: Its very special taste

YIXIANG: Will turn the bitter to the sweet.

(*speaks while tending the plants*) Nursing flowers, caring for plants, brewing wine, concocting medicine—since all these I do willingly, they present no hardship for me.

XINGYUAN: (*speaks*) That makes perfect sense. It's never painful to pursue what one feels like doing. Now that I'm free, allow me to help you attend the garden.

XINGYUAN *steps forward to assist* YIXIANG, *who, all smiles, shows him how to trim the trees, water the plants. . . . They seem to get along very well.*

[Chorus, *offstage*]

How very fortunate, when two show mutual
admiration, when flora are appreciated.
They've hit it off, hit it off, imagination running
wild, running wild.

Light fades out.

Scene 3: Getting Acquainted

West chamber of the Palace of Jingnan.
Huamei is seen chatting with three maidservants, downstage right.

HUAMEI: What exactly is the illness that bothers your young master?

MAIDSERVANTS 1 & 2: (*humming and hawing*) Er . . . it's . . . it's . . .

MAIDSERVANT 3: (*cutting in*) It's a very serious disease!

MAIDSERVANTS 1 & 2: Yes, right, very serious, very serious!

HUAMEI: How very serious?

MAIDSERVANT 1: Er . . .

MAIDSERVANT 2: (*cutting in*) More serious than the plague!

MAIDSERVANT 3: (*cutting in*) A kind of dementia!

HUAMEI: Ah? What exactly is it?

MAIDSERVANT 1: (*doing her best to explain it away*) It's dementia caused by the Double Plague.

MAIDSERVANTS 2 & 3: (*chiming in*) Yes, yes, really very serious!

MAIDSERVANT 1: (*adds*) Highly contagious!

HUAMEI: (*incredulous*) Dementia, and it's contagious? This is unheard of!

MAIDSERVANT 2: It's a new strain.

MAIDSERVANT 3: It's epidemic only in our country, not yet spread to Xuanwu . . .

HUAMEI: Ah? What?

Enter NANNY QIAO *on a walking stick.*

NANNY QIAO: What are you silly girls chattering about here
behind my back?
(*sees* HUAMEI) Oh, it's you, Huamei. How has the
Princess been these days?

HUAMEI: Well. Thank you.

MAIDSERVANT 3: I'm on my way to the garden to pick some
flowers. (*hurries off*)

MAIDSERVANT 1: The chief housekeeper wants me to get some
silk from the Dongnuan annex. I've got to run. (*hurries off*)

MAIDSERVANT 2: Er, I'll go see if the tailor is here. (*hurries off*)

NANNY QIAO: (*shouting from behind*) Diligence! No playing
around …

HUAMEI: Nanny Qiao, how is your young master doing after all?
My Princess is very much concerned.

NANNY QIAO: This illness of his, well, . . . is nothing serious. A
couple of days of quiet rest and he'll be OK.

HUAMEI: How do you know?

NANNY QIAO: Well, I just visited him.

HUAMEI: What? Nanny Qiao, aren't you afraid to catch the disease?

NANNY QIAO: Catch what disease?

HUAMEI: Dementia, of course!

NANNY QIAO: Ha, ha! In my whole life I've never heard that
dementia is contagious. Ha, ha! Besides, my young
master . . . (*suddenly alarmed*) Whoever told you that he
has dementia?

HUAMEI: I heard it from some of the maids here (*says the following
in one breath*) that the young master suffers from a
powerfully contagious dementia that results from the
Double Plague. Why aren't you afraid?

NANNY QIAO: (*embarrassed*) Er, well . . . I dance every day, so
I've got a perfect immune system.

HUAMEI: Ai! Nanny Qiao, stop this fooling around. We've been
here for many days, and we haven't seen the young prince.
Nor do we know what's going on. Instead of being allowed
into the nuptial chamber, we're ushered into the west
chamber. This is preposterous! My lady is very upset. Early
this morning she ordered me to start packing. We'll be
leaving soon, I am sure.

NANNY QIAO: Oh, no! That must not be!

HUAMEI: Her ladyship is a precious jewel. She can never
countenance the slightest wrong. Once she becomes willful,
nobody can dissuade her. Well, well, I have to go in. I
haven't done the packing yet. (*turns and enters the room,
pretending to be putting things in order*)

NANNY QIAO: (*aside*) Aiya! This is terrible! The young master is missing, and nobody knows his whereabouts. Even though His Highness has made an excuse of illness, this can only fool the Princess for a short while. Now she seems to have grown suspicious. This is a serious matter! I'll report it to His Highness immediately. (*rushes off*)

HUAMEI: (*runs to the door to see* NANNY QIAO *leave*) Hee, hee! Soon the truth will be known.

Enter two LADIES-IN-WAITING, *preceding* PRINCESS YULAN *assisted by* HUAMEI.

[Female chorus, *offstage*]:

> **In mincing steps the lovely lady walks.**
> **Sweet scent she wafts, her shadows dance.**
> **At flow'ring age, unparalleled in splendor,**
> **Our nation's pride, she far outdoes the peony.**

Behind THE PRINCESS *stand the two* LADIES-IN-WAITING; HUAMEI *waiting on at the side.*
THE PRINCESS *is reading attentively, occasionally gasping in admiration.*

PRINCESS: (*sings*)

> **For days on end I've been all entranced,**

Neglecting springtime's beauty, flowers' scents,

All due to this wise collection, *Watching High Tides*,

   of insight rare;

Each piece excels in theme and form.

Its subtlety and genius are beyond all praise;

Its principles profound and prescient.

As I reflect on them I can't conceal my high regard:

A work of highest merit leaves me deep in thought.

HUAMEI: Since your ladyship chanced upon this book, you've been hugging it, reading it day and night. What is this book?

PRINCESS: How could you conceive? This collection of verse is splendid in imagination and sublimely musical. Its content shows the author's wide range of knowledge ancient and modern. Deep meaning is couched in approachable language. Indeed, this deserves to be called the best book by the greatest talent of the world!

HUAMEI: Who wrote it?

PRINCESS: There's no name on it. (*glances at the volume*) The style is quite classical. It doesn't look like a contemporary work. I would have liked to meet the author, but . . .

HUAMEI: Since it's found here, your ladyship can ask the Prince of Jingnan. He should know.

PRINCESS: Well.

THE PRINCESS *goes on with her reading, occasionally pointing at the page and chatting with* HUAMEI, *who looks toward the door from time to time.*

SHIYUAN: (*sings offstage*)

A strange turn of events has come to pass,

(*enters, continues singing*)

Abruptly rose huge waves in a calm lake.

Concerned about my disappearing brother,

I have to soothe the Princess, calm my father.

The truth cannot be told;

With craft I'll try t' explain.

HUAMEI: (*walks to the door to look around; bursts out laughing*)

Just as I guessed!

SHIYUAN: (*folding his hands in salutation*) Miss Huamei, please inform Her Highness the Princess that I crave audience on business.

HUAMEI: Please wait a moment, sir. (*enters the room*)

Your Highness, the younger master of Jingnan craves an audience.

PRINCESS: Show him in.

HUAMEI *goes out, shows* SHIYUAN *into the room.*

SHIYUAN: (*saluting*) My respects to Your Highness.

PRINCESS: You may sit.

SHIYUAN: Thank you. (*sits down*)

HUAMEI: Your Honor must have come to talk about young master's illness. Her Highness has been waiting for some time.

SHIYUAN: (*very awkwardly*) Well . . .

PRINCESS: (*concerned*) Well? What kind of illness?

SHIYUAN: it's . . . er . . .

HUAMEI: What is it? Tell us!

PRINCESS: Is it serious?

SHIYUAN: Er, not really.

PRINCESS: (*incredulous*) Really? Perhaps Your Honor would rather keep it a secret?

She waves off HUAMEI *and the other* LADIES-IN-WAITING.

PRINCESS: Well?

SHIYUAN: (*sincerely*) I dare not deceive Your Highness. My elder brother, in fact—it would be improper to explain at this moment. In any case, we entreat Your Highness to stay on for a few more days, and my father will surely give a full account.

PRINCESS: Oh? (*looks at* SHIYUAN *in the eye; pauses*) If that's the case, I won't press it for the time being.

SHIYUAN: I am much obliged to Your Highness. (*pauses*) My father, seeing that you must be tired after such a long journey, wonders whether you find the accommodations and food here agreeable. If you need anything, our servants are at your command.

PRINCESS: It's very considerate of you to enquire. Those things do not really matter, but I would like you to enlighten me on one thing.

SHIYUAN: You're too polite. Please name it.

PRINCESS: (*picking up the book*) Do you know who wrote this collection, *Watching High Tides*?

SHIYUAN: (*taken aback*) Ah? Why does Your Highness ask about it?

PRINCESS: I found the book by chance, and once I started reading I just could not put it down. The author is one of great intelligence and sagacity. How admirable!

SHIYUAN: Ya!—

(*sings an aside*)

Last year in idleness sensing the spinning of the world,

I penned these verses to express my thoughts.

A small volume 'tis to amuse like-minded friends.

Who'd know a kindred spirit is right here.

The lovely princess' earnestness abashes me,

Yet I will open up and freely speak my mind.

(*speaks*) I'm ashamed to admit that this is my humble work.

PRINCESS: (*pleasantly surprised*) Oh, pardon my ineptitude. I
    didn't know the author was close at hand.

SHIYUAN: The judicious will sneer at my sloppy work.

PRINCESS: You need not be so humble. These verses exhibit the
    author's lofty goals. His great concern for the country and
    its people is apparent on every page. What was the occasion
    of the book, may I ask?

SHIYUAN: Allow me to explain, Your Highness:
    (*sings*)

> **Baihu, the land of the White Tiger, its army
>   fortified,**
> **Provoked us on the border at year's end.**
> **With rampant floods in northern Su District,**
> **His Majesty refrained from charging into war.**
> **And yet appeasement nothing shows but weakness,**
> **And leads to more aggression, not enduring peace.**

PRINCESS: (*sings*)

> **Indeed a frightful bully is Baihu;**
> **Early this year it also struck Xuanwu.**
> **Although His Majesty my father is too old to lodge**
> **A complaint, yet day and night it worries me.**
> **What course do you propose that we should take?**
> **Tell me and together we'll assessment make.**

SHIYUAN: In my humble opinion—

(*sings*)

> First come people, then the sovereign king.
>
> Encouragement of agriculture tops th' agenda.
>
> Give people time to rest: reduce their tax,
>
> Wipe out corruption, form a moral government.

They go on to sing in duet.

PRINCESS: It takes stability at home to fend off foes abroad.

Promote the worthy to help rule the land.

SHIYUAN: When granaries are filled with crops,

Enlist civilians for the troops.

PRINCESS: If citizens' morale is high,

SHIYUAN: We can with ease encroachers crush!

PRINCESS: (*happy*) Exactly! I agree.

How, then, shall our two countries closely cooperate, to teach our enemy a lesson?

SHIYUAN: That won't be difficult. (*pointing at the huge map on the wall*) First you may station your troops at Yenmen, and then take the route of Taihang; our soldiers will march from Xiangyang and go straight to Xianyang. In this way simultaneously attacking from north and south . . .

The two start a discussion, gesturing variously and making military maneuvers on the sand table.

[Chorus, *offstage*]

> **A destined meeting unarranged can bring**
>
> **More joy than union after separation long.**
>
> **He glows while speaking on and on;**
>
> **She answers with soft words and winsome smiles.**
>
> **Thus trading views on national security,**
>
> **Two thinking ones their first acquaintance make.**

Re-enter HUAMEI, *peeking.*

HUAMEI: How very odd! What exactly does the young master suffer from? Why isn't Her Highness worried at all?

Light dims.

Scene 4: The Escape

Peach Blossom Valley. YIXIANG'S *chamber.*
Night. OLD MAN *and* YIXIANG *are talking.*

OLD MAN: . . . Tomorrow, at a quarter after eleven, (*retrieving a vial from his bosom*) mix this with wine and get him to drink it. That's all there is to it. This is of great importance and must not be delayed!

YIXIANG: This . . . Ah (*shocked*), arsenic! This is poison! Why . . . ?

OLD MAN: (*harshly*) Don't ask, just do as you're told.

YIXIANG: But this will take his life!

OLD MAN: (*resolutely*) Exactly—take his life!

YIXIANG: But Master, didn't you say he is our honored guest and must be treated with respect? Didn't you say you'd send him back on the fifteenth? Why instead do you want to . . .? What has he done wrong?

OLD MAN: Yixiang, it is not his fault. It's just that the situation has changed, and your master has no other choice.

YIXIANG: These days, while trapped here, he's been watering flowers and pruning trees—all without one word of complaint . . .

OLD MAN: What of that?

YIXIANG: Is there no other alternative, Master?

OLD MAN: A great enterprise must not be turned awry by even one drop of the milk of human kindness.

YIXIANG: A great enterprise? What great enterprise is it that could make you take his life?

Lost in thought, OLD MAN *is silent.*

YIXIANG: Master, (*kneels*) I beg you, spare him. You see, the terrain of Peach Blossom Valley is precipitous, with devices ingeniously deployed. There's no way he can get out of here. Why kill an innocent person?

OLD MAN: He innocent? Humph! That's because you are ignorant. The blood debt of past generations is in him. He was born with this original sin, which (*thinks for a moment*) you don't understand.

YIXIANG: I—I—I just can't do it. Master, I've never disobeyed you before, but, to kill someone . . . especially someone who is . . .

OLD MAN: An enemy!

YIXIANG: What? What did you say?

OLD MAN: All right, Yixiang. Perhaps the time has come for me to tell you the truth.

YIXIANG: The truth?

OLD MAN: (*nodding slowly*) Yes! The truth is extremely cruel. It is a secret that I've kept for many years.

Come, sit down, and listen to me.

OLD MAN *helps* YIXIANG *up, and the two sit on a stone chair.*

OLD MAN: (*sings*)

> Fifteen years ago, in alliance Canglong and
> Xuanwu
> With powerful forces surprise-attacked Zhuque,
> Whose emperor and empress died one after the
> other;
> So sudden came the strike, all over corpses lay.
> The little princess at her bosom, the worn-out
> Nurse
> From place to place sought out somewhere to hide.
> By chance staying in an ancient temple,
> I took the princess from the dying nurse.

YIXIANG: Ah—you mean . . . I was the . . .

OLD MAN: (*nodding*) Yes, that you were. Later I went into exile with you, till three years ago we came to this Peach Blossom Valley.

YIXIANG: Ah, so you are not just my master; you saved my life!

OLD MAN: Yixiang—no, I mean, Your Highness—in fact, I once served as your father's chief commander of the imperial

guards . . . I failed to protect the royal house and deserve to
die ten thousand deaths! I've sinned against the Empire of
Zhuque!

YIXIANG: Oh Master!

OLD MAN: All these years I've been watching in secret, hoping that
one day I might take revenge. Now the opportunity has
come. . . .

YIXIANG: Ancient grudge—what does that have to do with *him*?

OLD MAN: Who do you think it was that led the joined forces to
attack Zhuque?

YIXIANG: Who?

OLD MAN: None other than the Prince of Jingnan! His high position
he got at the expense of our country and our families!

YIXIANG: O heavens! And yet, why don't you go kill the Prince of
Jingnan? It was he who was responsible.

OLD MAN: Well, of course you couldn't have known. When they
struck the alliance, the Emperor of Canglong adopted the
Prince of Jingnan's elder son, and prearranged the marriage
between him and Xuanwu's princess, to strengthen the tie.
The time has come now for them to get ready for the big
joyous occasion, but I kidnapped the bridegroom, and left
in his name a letter declining the marriage. Isn't this a
perfect strategy to cause trouble and sabotage their alliance?

YIXIANG: Ah! Master, you . . .

OLD MAN: This would be a sweeter revenge than just murdering the Prince of Jingnan!

In order to steal something written in his elder son's hand, I've risked my life several times to sneak into Jingnan Palace. Now, I don't want my plan to fall through at the last minute!

YIXIANG: Now that you have detained him in the Valley, you must already have wreaked havoc in the world outside and achieved your goal. Why do you have to kill him?

OLD MAN: No, the goal . . . has not been achieved: that's the problem. I don't know why, but outside . . . all is very quiet and peaceful. Therefore, I must kill him to raise havoc.

YIXIANG: Well, Master . . .

OLD MAN: No more of this. Just follow the plan.

YIXIANG: Well, I . . .

OLD MAN: Yixiang, remember well that this enmity is irreconcilable.

It's getting late. Don't let your imagination run wild. Go to bed now! Tomorrow will be a busy day. Understand?

YIXIANG: Master . . .

OLD MAN: (*pats* YIXIANG *on the shoulder*) All right, go. (*exit*)

YIXIANG: O heavens! What should I do?

[Chorus, *offstage*]:

> The homeland shattered, families dispersed,
> The loss of parents pains her year on year.

YIXIANG: (*sings*)

> A millstone are my Master's words, and in
> A trice this dale's no more a Shangri-La.
> The sky is whirling, the earth twirling,
> And my heart shivers in this heartless cold.
> Kind words evap'rate in a blink;
> Deep-rooted hatred just won't go away.
> My indecisive mind is running mad;
> Throughout the moon-lit night I lie awake.

She paces, ponders, stares at the vial, again ponders and paces.

YIXIANG: (*speaks*) I cannot disobey Master . . . besides, the hatred of generations . . .

[Chorus, *offstage*]:

> Hostility, injustice, hate, of nation and of family—
> The debt of blood needs must be paid in blood.

YIXIANG: (*on second thought, speaks*) But His Honor . . .

> (*sings*)

> He's honest, natural, and generous of mind,
> His manner humble, calm, and so polite,

I can't but fall in love with him in secrecy:
I could have stitched a pair of lovebirds on my
** scarf.**
These days he seems to wish to tell me something,
His eyes gleam with affection, yet his words fall
** short.**
Now I see a golden marriage long has been
** arranged,**
My sadness I can only keep in quiet to myself.
And yet though out of hope to be his spouse,
I cannot bear to be his murderer, and take his life.

(*speaks*) No, no, I can't . . . (*resolved*) Alas! Even if I have
to bear the ill name of traitor to my country and my house,
I'll protect him! (*exit in a rush*)

[Chorus, *female voice offstage*]:
The hourglass shows sand at the fifth watch,
The day's about to break, the rain has stopped.

Re-enter YIXIANG *in a hurry, followed by* XINGYUAN.
They mime walking up and down slopes, crossing the
stream, avoiding deployed devices such as golden-armored
robot warriors and the eighteen warrior-monks. From time
to time smoke permeates the stage and blasts of dynamite
are heard.

[Chorus, *offstage, continues*]:

(*Female voice*)

> **In such a hurry, scenery holds no appeal;**
>
> **With great alarm, we rush to leave the dale.**

(*Male voice*)

> **Never mind the early spring so chill and wet,**
>
> **Never mind high hills and water deep.**

(*Female voice*)

> **Never mind the winding paths all muddied up,**

(*Male voice*)

> **Never mind the murkiness and traps close by.**

(*Together*)

> **Though fearful, apprehensive, we yet keep our**
>
> **calm,**
>
> **Meandering through labyrinths with cautious steps.**

Armored robot warriors pop up one by one around them.
They fight back with swords, demonstrating various
postures and motions appropriate to swordsmanship.
Finally, XINGYUAN *"kills" a warrior with one thrust.*

XINGYUAN: (*pulls* YIXIANG) Let's go!

OLD MAN *suddenly enters, trying to stop them.*

OLD MAN: (*shouts angrily*) Where are you going? (*thrusting his* *sword toward* XINGYUAN) Take this!

YIXIANG: (*rushing forward, she fends off* OLD MAN'S *sword with hers*) Master!

(*turns her head back and shouts at* XINGYUAN) Run away quick!

XINGYUAN: (*hesitant*) Yixiang!

OLD MAN: (*keeps attacking*) Out of my way!

YIXIANG: (*keeps fending off her master's sword*) Never mind me, just go!

XINGYUAN: You take care! (*turns and rushes off*)

OLD MAN *is about to chase him.*

YIXIANG: (*throwing down her sword, steps forward to tug at* OLD MAN *and kneels down*) Master!

OLD MAN: You—you . . . (*stamps his foot and gives a long sigh*) Ai—!

Light dims.

(Intermission)

Scene 5: Soul-searching

The Flowered Hall of Jingnan Palace.
MAIDSERVANTS 1 *and* 2 at work.

MAIDSERVANT 1: (*mopping tables and chairs*) . . . So the young
    master was kidnapped!

MAIDSERVANT 2: (*pasting words of blessing*) Who could've
    imagined such things!

    Enter MAIDSERVANT 3 *with a bunch of flowers.*

MAIDSERVANT 3: (*arranging flowers*) What have you been
    chatting about?

MAIDSERVANT 1: Well, we were saying that our young master . . .

MAIDSERVANT 2: I wonder who would be so foolishly brave,
    tickling the tiger's teeth by entering the palace to kidnap
    him!

MAIDSERVANT 1: Surely His Grace the Prince will get to the
    bottom of the matter?

MAIDSERVANT 3: I just heard that he has commanded that
    General Ke lead a troop to arrest the traitors.

MAIDSERVANT 1: Where to catch them?

MAIDSERVANT 3: I didn't hear it clearly. Sounded like Peach

Blossom Village or Plum Blossom Hill . . .

MAIDSERVANT 2: Luckily the young master is back safe and sound.

MAIDSERVANT 1: Heaven and earth be praised!

MAIDSERVANT 3: Well, tomorrow is the big day. Are the flower decorations in the nuptial chamber all in pairs?

MAIDSERVANT 1: I don't know. All day I've been busy working here. I haven't had time to step into the nuptial chamber yet.

MAIDSERVANT 2: Nor have I checked it. . . .

MAIDSERVANT 3: Aiya! We have to hurry to make sure then, or Nanny Qiao will certainly scream at us . . . .

Exeunt.

Enter XINGYUAN.

Slides: showing XINGYUAN *and* YIXIANG *talking and laughing in Peach Blossom Valley.*

XINGYUAN: (*sings*)

> **In haste I left the Valley, home returned,**
> **Dejected, as if I'd something lost.**
> **With knitted brow, I coldly face the wedding day.**
> **Her looks by Peach Blossom Creek haunt me still.**
> **Shoulder to shoulder did we pick plantains on the**
> **   hill;**
> **When warming wine we leaned against each other**

close.

All this, like a dream, how can one record?

Once past, the time will leave no trace.

I ne'er know blinding passion in this world

Till, unaware, I jot down words of yearning love.

(*speaks*) Alas, this golden marriage by imperial and patriarchal command does not suit me; it just isn't right— (*continues to sing*)

Having turned it o'er, I'd like to speak my mind,

Yet how should I proceed to give my dad a clue?

Enter PRINCE OF JINGNAN and NANNY QIAO.

NANNY QIAO: (*pointing here and there*) See, my lord, isn't everything well done? With me overseeing, the maidservants wouldn't dare to lie down on the job! Here are flowers, firecrackers, silk balls—nothing auspicious is lacking. And also the rice-sieve, the charcoal-fire pot, and the nuptial wine: everything's ready.

PRINCE OF JINGNAN: Good. We can't be too careful regarding the ceremonial procedure.

NANNY QIAO: Sure, sure. (*catching sight of* XINGYUAN) Ah, my lord the young master! (*bows*) My lord the young master!

XINGYUAN: (*bows to his father*) Father!

PRINCE OF JINGNAN: Well. You've had it tough these days.

XINGYUAN: It's OK. (*hesitant*) Father, er . . .

NANNY QIAO: Young master, are you so worried that you have to come inspect in person? Come, come, with me in charge, you may well rest in peace!

XINGYUAN: Much obliged, Nanny Qiao. I, er . . .

PRINCE OF JINGNAN: Well? What is it?

XINGYUAN: (*determined*) My dear Father—

> (*sings*)
>
> **Imperial favor boundless has this marriage given,**
> **Great fortune like this one should fast embrace.**
> **Yet what I have gone through no trifle is,**
> **I've mulled it over since returning home.**
> **I beg of you this marriage to postpone,**
> **More carefully let's weigh it for the best.**

NANNY QIAO: (*aside*) My goodness! Tsk, tsk, tsk, what is he talking about?

PRINCE OF JINGNAN: (*flicks his sleeve in show of anger*) Tut! Nonsense!

> (*sings*)
>
> **What flight of fancy wild is this the order to**
> **disturb!**
> **You would deceive your lord with trash like this!**
> **In boundless grace His Majesty the marriage has**
> **proclaimed;**

How can you disobey and change the date?

(*speaks*) This is ridiculous! Has it never occurred to you what a great bounty this marriage is? The alliance is sure to bring to our house unending wealth and prosperity!

XINGYUAN: But Father, to hold the ceremony in such a hurry cannot be appropriate. Let's put it off for a while and . . .

PRINCE OF JINGNAN: Silence! Perhaps you're bored with this life, eh, thus daring to bargain with His Majesty the Emperor?

XINGYUAN: How dare I? Please cease your anger, Father. It's only that . . .

PRINCE OF JINGNAN: You dare not? If so, then keep your mouth shut! Humph!

NANNY QIAO: (*keeps tipping him the wink*) Er, my young master, just mince your words. We cannot disobey an imperial command. And, your father has made enormous efforts preparing for the ceremony. Even we underlings have busied ourselves for the better part of a year to make sure everything is ready. Nobody's been idle. This ceremony has not been hurriedly prepared, but organized with the utmost care. Most young men are very nervous before a marriage and have such wild thoughts as yours. Don't worry, a good sleep and you'll be all right.

XINGYUAN: Well . . .

NANNY QIAO: (*stopping him*) All right, all right. Now I have to escort my lord your father to inspect the nuptial chamber. We're very busy. (*escorting the* PRINCE) My lord, as to the nuptial chamber, I've also made sure . . .

PRINCE OF JINGNAN: Humph.

NANNY QIAO: Scrolls, screens, pillows, blankets . . . all things for the marriage come in pairs. Extremely auspicious. I'm sure you'll be pleased. . . .

The PRINCE *gives* XINGYUAN *a look before he exits with* NANNY QIAO.

XINGYUAN: (*thinking aloud*) So, what's to be done? Father is adamant, but I shouldn't follow him like a fool. (*thinks for a moment, then makes up his mind*) All right, then! (*goes to the table and starts to write; sings*)

> **All undependable are wealth and worldly fame;**
> **They are no match for a bosom lady love.**
> **This message having left, from palace now will I**
> **   depart.**
> **I've searched my soul, searched my soul, I will not**
> **   hesitate!** (*Exit*)

Light dims.

Scene 6: Enamored

The west chamber of the Jingnan Palace.

Enter the PRINCESS.

PRINCESS: (*sings*)

One half worry and one half joy

Keep rippling in the lake that is my heart.

The cause of this I do not know,

But surely I myself have lost control.

I wish t'unload my mind in words,

And yet no verse can bear a love so deep.

Unceasing rain of spring does sympathize with me:

It keeps on dropping, like my endless yearning.

Enter HUAMEI *with a book for the* PRINCESS, *who receives it with a casual glance.*

PRINCESS: Alas! (*puts down the book on the table, nonchalantly*)

HUAMEI: Your Highness, after a long wait the wedding will take place tomorrow. Why then are you sighing?

PRINCESS: Well, you won't understand. . . .

HUAMEI: Are you unhappy that the Prince is not making the

ceremony splendid enough?

PRINCESS: (*shaking her head*) No.

HUAMEI: Or that the young master has not come to visit you?

PRINCESS: (*shaking her head*) No.

HUAMEI: Not this nor that—ah, now I know. Must have been thinking about . . . that person . . .

PRINCESS: No nonsense here!

Enter SHIYUAN, *with a pack and a long sword slung over his shoulder.*

SHIYUAN: (*sings*)

In flowers' shadow by west chamber up and down I pace.

A tree away an oriole at my silly passion mocks.

HUAMEI *looks out furtively.*

HUAMEI: Well, well, look, I wasn't talking nonsense. That person— is here!

PRINCESS: Which person? (*rises*)

HUAMEI: (*pointing to outside of the window*) Who else?

PRINCESS: Ya! (*delighted*)

HUAMEI *gestures to the* PRINCESS, *who looks bashful.*

SHIYUAN: (*continues singing*)

> **Although in love, I need to hold my tongue.**
> **What pain it is to bid farewell tonight!**

HUAMEI *is just stepping out of the door when* SHIYUAN *arrives at the west chamber.*

SHIYUAN: Miss Huamei, please report my visit.

HUAMEI: Her Highness bids you come in.

SHIYUAN: How did she know I was coming?

HUAMEI: (*giggling*) Her sensitive mind can read yours!

SHIYUAN: Oh?

HUAMEI: This way please.

SHIYUAN *enters the chamber following* HUAMEI.

SHIYUAN: Your Highness.

PRINCESS: Your Honor.

PRINCESS: (*to* Huamei) Serve tea.

HUAMEI: Yes. (*exit*)

PRINCESS: (*sizing up* Shiyuan) Why are you dressed up like this?

SHIYUAN: To be honest, I'm here to bid you farewell.

PRINCESS: (*stunned*) Where are you going?

SHIYUAN: I've obtained from my father the permission to guard Xiangyang, to prevent invasions.

PRINCESS: When are you leaving?

SHIYUAN: This moment.

> HUAMEI *re-enters with a tea plate, serves tea, and stands by.*

PRINCESS: Why such a hurry?

SHIYUAN: Well . . .

> [Chorus, *offstage*]
>> **Affection deep now buried in the heart;**
>> **About to say it, yet he feels confused.**
>> **The sentiment there are not words enough to**
>>> **verbalize;**
>> **Each knows what's weighing on their minds.**

SHIYUAN: Sooner or later I have to leave. Better sooner.

PRINCESS: Your Honor!

SHIYUAN: (*as if in high spirits*) I'll go first, to get the weaponry in order, so that at Your Highness' command, we can destroy the invading Baihu! What do you think?

PRINCESS: (*forcing a cheerful look*) Well . . . that'd be fine.

SHIYUAN: I humbly take my leave.

PRINCESS: Do take care.

> *The* PRINCESS *watches* SHIYUAN *walk out of the chamber and then in tears exit, followed by* HUAMEI.

Slide: A scene from Scene Three ("Getting Acquainted") *where* PRINCESS *and* SHIYUAN *enjoyed a discussion on national defense.*

[Chorus, *offstage*]:
> **Affection deep now buried in the heart,**
> **The Parting makes them both forlorn.**
> **With marriage hopelessly beyond his hold,**
> **Her graceful image he can only find in dreams, in**
> **dreams.**

SHIYUAN: (*sees the letter on the ground*) Well, what's this?

He picks it up and reads.

(XINGYUAN'S *voice, offstage*) "And yet, life is short and our days fleeting. In this life what should one look for? Nothing but a person of kindred spirit. Slow-witted though I am, I would hope to solve this life's puzzle. Thus am I emboldened to beg on my knees that you would retract your published command. . . ."

SHIYUAN: Oh no! Is Brother kidnapped again? What to do now?

Enter XINGYUAN *with a bag and a long sword slung over his shoulder, searching for something on the road.*

XINGYUAN: (*anxious, thinking aloud*) Alas, where could I have lost it? How come it's nowhere to be found?

SHIYUAN: (*surprised to see* XINGYUAN; *aside*) Well! Lucky he wasn't kidnapped! What's going on? He just got back; why is he going on a journey again?

XINGYUAN: (*sees* SHIYUAN) Oh, no! (*hurries to cover up his travel bag*)

SHIYUAN: Brother, where are you going?

XINGYUAN: Where are *you* going, may I ask?

SHIYUAN: I have received command to guard the town of Xiangyang, remember?

XINGYUAN: Ah, (*tapping his forehead*) see how forgetful I am! (*embarrassed*) I, er . . . (*reaching out his hand*) give it to me.

SHIYUAN *hands him the letter, which* XINGYUAN *carefully puts away.*

SHIYUAN: Brother, tomorrow's the day of your joyful marriage with Princess Yulan, and you . . .?

XINGYUAN: Dear brother, since there's no hiding it, I might as well be honest with you. I cannot marry the Princess. . . .

SHIYUAN: (*shocked*) Ah? Why not?

XINGYUAN: Because . . . because there's someone else. (*about to go*)

SHIYUAN: No, Brother. (*stopping him*) By imperial decree, you must marry the Princess.

XINGYUAN: Get out of my way!

SHIYUAN: No. If you evade the problem by simply walking away, what's to happen to the Princess?

XINGYUAN: (*pushing* SHIYUAN *away*) That's not my concern.

SHIYUAN: (*blocking* XINGYUAN) You can't insult the Princess!

XINGYUAN: Out of my way! Or I'll have to resort to force.

SHIYUAN: No! You have to marry the Princess.

XINGYUAN: All right! See if you can keep me here.

They fight fiercely. Twice XINGYUAN *is able to get away, but twice* SHIYUAN, *risking his life, throws himself on his brother. All of a sudden,* XINGYUAN *leaps away.*

XINGYUAN: Stop! Since tomorrow is my wedding day, why do you pick this time to leave for Xiangyang?

SHIYUAN: Well, I . . . Ah, dear Brother—I might as well tell you the truth, too.

(*sings*)

While you were missing, chaos ruled the palace.

Sent on a mission to assuage Her Highness,

I fell in love with her—a huge mistake!

I'll leave to put an end to such a fancy.

XINGYUAN: (*surprised*) Oh! (*a thought occurs to him; smilingly*) So that's why. Now I have an idea that might do both of us good.

SHIYUAN: What do you mean?

XINGYUAN: My dear brother—(*They sing a duet.*)

By nature free of care and unadventurous,

I'd rather stay in country and forgo ceremonies.

The elder son conventional must ever be;

Rulership's restraint is hard for me to bear.

SHIYUAN: How could you utter words like these?

This marriage by His Majesty is fixed;

To break the contract will surely lead to enmity,

Nor can you have peace of mind if you forsake the

Princess.

XINGYUAN: In Peach Blossom Valley have I true love found;

The firstborn's rights I yield to you.

In alliance you can formulate good policies,

And use your talent to establish lasting peace.

SHIYUAN: Far be such wild fancy from my mind;

Heaven knows my truthful heart!

XINGYUAN: High heaven has it all well planned;

With polished grace it shows you to the bloom.

SHIYUAN: (*speaks*) Well, er . . .

(*sings*)

I wonder whether she'll consent.

This does require careful thought.

XINGYUAN: **As urgency demands a prompt decision, brother**
dear,
Act now, and tell Her Highness this good news!

SHIYUAN: But I just bade her farewell!

XINGYUAN: It doesn't matter. Go again, just deliver another speech.
Dear brother, Father has already dispatched an army to
Peach Blossom Valley. I've got to get there immediately.
(*smilingly, retrieves the letter*) I was about to leave this
letter in the library, but now I'll trouble you to present it to
Father.

SHIYUAN: (*takes the letter*): Dear brother . . .

XINGYUAN: We'll meet again someday. (*looking at* SHIYUAN *in*
the eye)

SHIYUAN: (*looking at* XINGYUAN *in the eye*) You take care.

XINGYUAN: You, too.

After a parting salutation, they exit in different directions.

Light dims.

Scene 7: No Regret

The bottom of Peach Blossom Valley.

GENERAL KE *rushes on with his troops.*

GENERAL KE: (*to the tune of* "Jiji Feng") Attention: Let's attack
    Peach Blossom Valley! It's the Prince's command that we
    take them alive!

GUARDS: Yes!

> *Smoke fills the stage; devices such as golden-armored
> warriors frequently pop up to fight with* GENERAL KE *and
> his men. Enter* OLD MAN *and* YIXIANG, *who are defeated.*

OLD MAN: (*looking around*) I knew there would be such a day, so
    I've had a boat ready. . . . Come, let's get on board. Be
    careful!

> GENERAL KE *and his men rush up to stop them.*

GENERAL KE: Running away? That won't be easy! (*swings his
    sword*)

YIXIANG: (*shouts in alarm*): Master!

OLD MAN: (*parries, then sends it back*) Ha, ha! Just the few of you, to stop me?

GENERAL KE: Let's see then.

They circle OLD MAN. YIXIANG *is about to flick her sleeve.*

GENERAL KE: (*snatches* YIXIANG) Behave yourself, lady! No tranquilizer tricks!

YIXIANG: Ah!

OLD MAN: (*parrying, concerned*) Are you all right, Yixiang?

GENERAL KE: Old man, put your sword down and surrender, and this lady will be spared.

OLD MAN: And, if I refuse?

GENERAL KE: I'll cut her into eight parts!

OLD MAN: Monster! (*rushing toward* KE *with a whack*)

GENERAL KE: (*pushes* YIXIANG *to some guards*) Tie her up!

(*guards tie up* YIXIANG *while* KE *has several more bouts with* OLD MAN)

Eh? This is . . . Zhuque method?

OLD MAN: Ha, ha! Very discerning!

GENERAL KE: Who are you?

OLD MAN: Never mind! Take this! (*attacking fast*)

GENERAL KE: Hold it! (*leaping away*) These two moves, "Peacock in Full Display" and "Right on Peacock's Eyes," are taught only to imperial kinsmen. Who are you after all?

OLD MAN: Humph! Shut up! (*attacking aggressively*)

GENERAL KE: Attack him, everyone! He must not escape!

> OLD MAN, *encircled and losing strength, takes a hit on the right arm from* KE.

OLD MAN: (*dropping his sword, pressing the wound with his left hand*) Ah!

> *The guards tightly surround* OLD MAN, *with their swords pointing toward him.*

OLD MAN: (*in frustration*) Alas, the heavens would destroy me. It's fate!

> *He suddenly grabs with his left hand a sword from a guard and is about to commit suicide.*
> *Enter* XINGYUAN *with a leap. He beats away* OLD MAN'S *sword.*

XINGYUAN: Stop! (*pointing his sword in a circle to turn back the guards*)

GUARDS: (*paying respect*) Your lordship!

XINGYUAN: General Ke, I have command from my father to take care of this. Now I order you to leave Peach Blossom Valley at once!

GENERAL KE: (*he and the guards look at each other dumbfounded*)

Well, er . . .

XINGYUAN: Well? Dare you disobey the command?

GENERAL KE: Your servant dare not. And yet His Highness the Prince said earlier to arrest the traitors in the valley and have them interrogated at the palace. I just discovered that (*pointing to* OLD MAN) this man seems to be a survivor of the evil Zhuque Empire . . . As this is a matter of great consequence, I . . .

XINGYUAN: Oh, yeah? (*looks at* OLD MAN, *and then at* YIXIANG) That's nonsense! Zhuque has long been extinct. What proof do you have?

GENERAL KE: Your lordship, this man uses his sword in methods closely guarded by the royal house of Zhuque. No outsiders could have known them.

XINGYUAN: Is that so? It's quite common for hereditary martial tactics to leak out. We must not make wild assumptions. General Ke, lend me your ears. (*stepping forward with* GENERAL KE, *in low voice*) In fact, my father has given me another mission, which I can't tell you at this moment. Do retreat now.

GENERAL KE: In that case, I humbly take my leave. (*waving his hand, he exits with the guards*)

XINGYUAN *rushes forward to untie* YIXIANG.

XINGYUAN: I came too late. You're not hurt, are you?

YIXIANG: Thank you very much for rescuing us. My master was wounded in the arm.

XINGYUAN: (*concerned*) How serious is it?

OLD MAN: Humph! No need to shed your crocodile tears! If it hadn't been for you, these guards wouldn't have been here! How could they have gained entrance to the Valley?

XINGYUAN: Please cease your anger, Master. That indeed was my fault. But once I learned that my father had dispatched skilled fighters, I travelled day and night to get here, lest something unfortunate should happen. . . .

YIXIANG: Why has your lordship come back?

OLD MAN: Are you not afraid that I might kill you? Better return home and make preparations for your wedding!

XINGYUAN: Well . . . To be honest with you, I've renounced my firstborn rights, and will never go back.

OLD MAN: (*shocked*) What?

YIXIANG: (*shocked*) Why?

XINGYUAN: (*in earnest*) Yixiang, since my return to the palace—
(*sings*)

> **Beneath red candles, nightly have I stayed awake;**
> **By ornate windows, all alone I gazed at the curved moon.**
> **Entranced, all I heard was "Temple Incantation".**

> Fair lady, your frowns and smiles kept haunting
> me.
> You of my dream, I knew I'd loved you for some
> time.
> Both rights of firstborn and royal marriage I
> forsook,
> And to His Highness in a letter explanation made.
> To be forever on a boat with you is all I wish!

(*kneeling down before* OLD MAN, *speaks*) May you grant my wish!

YIXIANG: (*touched*) You . . . (*turning to* OLD MAN; *also kneels down*) Master—

(*sings*)

> Absurdities abound here in this world;
> Tit for tat, retaliation never ends.
> You may be calculating as you can, but lose
> More than you gain: Is that so wise?

XINGYUAN: (*continues to sing*)

> All this will fill the tavern tales in ages hence,
> E'en as unblemished clouds float leisurely on.

YIXIANG: (*speaks*) Master, please—

YIXIANG AND XINGYUAN: (*together*)

> Make friends, not enemies;
> Let bygones be bygones.

OLD MAN: (*looks at* XINGYUAN, *and then at* YIXIANG; *to* XINGYUAN) Is all that you just said true?

XINGYUAN: I swear by heaven, not a word of falsehood.

OLD MAN: Will you not regret giving up fame and prosperity, betraying your house and country? Are you not worried about having to bear the infamy of disloyalty and unfilialness? Can you put up with a life of coarse clothes and lean meals?

XINGYUAN: (*looking at* YIXIANG) Yixiang once said, as long as one is willing, the greatest hardship is nothing. (*to* OLD MAN) Master, I am willing. Honestly.

OLD MAN: Providence! (*looking up at the heaven*) All is providence! Let be!

(*to* XINGYUAN) Your lordship, I mean, Xingyuan, take good care of Yixiang, or I'll never forgive you!

XINGYUAN: You can trust me, Master!

YIXIANG: Thank you very much, Master!

OLD MAN: Get up, both of you.

They stand up, with XINGYUAN *assisting* YIXIANG.

XINGYUAN: Master, what I told those soldiers was simply a guile to make them withdraw. Soon they'll surely be back. It's impossible to remain in Peach Blossom Valley any longer.

OLD MAN: Don't worry. Come, I've made preparations.

Assisting each other, the three board the boat. XINGYUAN
unties the rope and rows ahead.

[Chorus, *offstage*]:

Atop the charming mountains clouds appear,
And drooping willows line the bank, a serene sight.
Peach blossoms turn to look with winsome smiles:
From now on wind and moon no sadness will evoke,
no sadness will evoke.

Exeunt, slowly.

Light dims.

Scene 8: Marriage Declined

Late at night. The Flowered Hall of Jingnan palace.

PRINCE OF JINGNAN *in wrath.*

PRINCE OF JINGNAN: (*the letter in his hand*) . . . Absurd!
Absolutely absurd! Disloyal and unfilial! A clear case of
betrayal! Betraying both His Majesty the Emperor and me
his own father, he has not the slightest regard for family or
country. Left just like that. How am I going to face His
Majesty and the Emperor of Xuanwu?

SHIYUAN: Please cease your anger, Father. Before leaving, Brother
has asked that . . .

PRINCE OF JINGNAN: (*snapping at* SHIYUAN) And I'm shocked
by what you did! You didn't stop him but instead gave him
a hand! Now you're happy! In the grand wedding ceremony,
with all the dignitaries assembled, the bridegroom is
nowhere to be found—what's going to happen to my
dignity?

SHIYUAN: Father, Princess Yulan—

PRINCE OF JINGNAN: Right, the Princess! How am I going to
explain to the Princess? What new excuse do I have this

time? Could I again say he's ill? No matter how gracious she is, the Princess won't accept this! Humph! Such an unfilial son! To give up his firstborn rights and throw away prosperity that's proffered him—what could have bedeviled him?

SHIYUAN: Father, Brother had no other choice. He—

PRINCE OF JINGNAN: Silence! "There are laws in the nation and rules in the family." His willfulness shan't be tolerated! Guard!

Enter GUARD 1.

GUARD 1: Here, my lord.

PRINCE OF JINGNAN: Go to Peach Blossom Valley immediately and tell General Ke this order from my own mouth to have that unfilial son arrested and brought to me!

GUARD 1: Yes, Your Highness. (*exit*)

Enter NANNY QIAO, *who almost bumps into* GUARD 1.

NANNY QIAO: Aiyo! What's the matter? Why such a hurry . . . (*looks at the* PRINCE, *and then at* SHIYUAN) My lord, why are you so angry?

PRINCE OF JINGNAN: Humph! See for yourself, Nanny Qiao! (*hands her the letter*)

NANNY QIAO: (*takes the letter, looks at it right side up, and then* *turns it upside down*) Oh my goodness! Your Highness has forgotten that I can't read. (*examines the letter again*) And yet, it looks like Xingyuan's handwriting. (*turns it upside down again and looks at it*) Why does it look exactly the same as last time? Oh, no! Another forged letter! (*nervous*) The young master has been kidnapped again! No wonder I've been nervous all day long . . .

SHIYUAN: Nanny Qiao, this letter is not forged. Brother did run away this time . . .

NANNY QIAO: What? Where did he go? Why didn't he tell me?

PRINCE OF JINGNAN: Humph! He kept it even from me . . .

NANNY QIAO: (*suddenly remembers*) Aiya! What about the wedding tomorrow?

SHIYUAN: The Princess . . .

Enter GUARD 2.

GUARD 2: (*announces*) My lord, Princess Yulan is here. (*exit*)

PRINCE OF JINGNAN: Oh, God! Well . . . (*holding out his hands*) Leave us.

ALL: Yes, my lord. (*exeunt*)

PRINCE OF JINGNAN *hurries out to welcome* PRINCESS YULAN, *who is preceded by two* LADIES-IN-WAITING *and followed by* HUAMEI.

PRINCE OF JINGNAN: (*nervous*) My apologies for not giving
Your Highness a proper welcome. I didn't know you'd
come at this late hour.

PRINCESS: No need to stand on ceremony, my lord. (*having taken
a seat*) Please sit.

PRINCE OF JINGNAN: Thank you. (*he sits*)

PRINCESS: Does my lord know why I'm here?

PRINCE OF JINGNAN: (*fearful*) Well, er . . . no.

PRINCESS: Upon imperial command I have come here from the
north. On my way I've observed your land and people. You
have vast rice paddies and abundant crops; your people are
frank and pleasant. In my country, on the other hand, we
have throngs of cattle, and our people are skilled huntsmen
and warriors. Recently Baihu has often caused unrest along
the borders. An alliance between Canglong and Xuanwu
can benefit both countries, for we can supply each other
with what we have in abundance, and act in unity. My lord
understands this, I'm sure?

PRINCE OF JINGNAN: (*not knowing how to properly respond*)
Yes, yes, you're right.

PRINCESS: Precisely for that reason, the alliance between our two
countries is of the greatest importance.

PRINCE OF JINGNAN: Sure, sure.

PRINCESS: Should the alliance fall through, the consequences . . .

would be unthinkable.

PRINCE OF JINGNAN: (*frightened*) Please, Your Highness, enlighten me.

PRINCESS: In my opinion, the alliance is one thing; the nuptial league is quite another.

PRINCE OF JINGNAN: Ah?

PRINCESS: My lord—

(*sings*)

> **To marry by command of parents or by words of go-betweens,**
>
> **Thus leaving it to fate: it is a pity indeed.**
>
> **Since a spouse is meant to be a life companion,**
>
> **It's well to look with care for one's destined mate.**

PRINCE OF JINGNAN: Your Highness means . . . ?

PRINCESS: From the beginning of the world, we girls have never been our own mistresses but have had to bow to our fathers' will. And yet it's better—

(*continues in song*)

> **To do as one wishes, make one's choice;**
>
> **Better be a shattered jade than a tile kept whole.**
>
> **If time and tide wait not for man, let be;**
>
> **In the end lovely flow'rs will bloom in twain.**

PRINCE OF JINGNAN: (*faltering*) Well, er . . .

PRINCESS: (*calmly*) I never knew your elder son, and now we are luckless to see each other. If there's such ado even in a good thing, there's no need to force it. I have therefore decided to write to His Majesty my father, and depart for the north in three days.

PRINCE OF JINGNAN: Ah? Then what about . . . tomorrow . . . tomorrow . . .

PRINCESS: As for tomorrow (*in a faint smile*)—all's well, naturally. (*pauses*) I'm sure you can handle it properly.

PRINCE OF JINGNAN: Well, er . . . er . . .

PRINCESS: My lord, I have one more word.

PRINCE OF JINGNAN: I'm listening, Your Highness.

PRINCESS: His lordship your second son is a man of great talent and lofty goals, widely read and well-informed. Such a man is rare.

PRINCE OF JINGNAN: (*surprised*) Oh? Shiyuan?

PRINCESS: We are inclined to trouble him to escort us home, where we can discuss national defense. Would you grant our humble wish?

PRINCE OF JINGNAN: Ah? (*suddenly sees the point*) Oh, yes, yes, of course, of course. He shall be your escort. I'm deeply grateful to Your Highness for granting him this honor.

PRINCESS: (*smiles*) My lord, I believe our two nations can work together with one heart and keep our friendship forever.

PRINCE OF JINGNAN: Yes, thank you very much, Princess!

The drum strikes the third watch.

PRINCESS: It's already the third watch of the night. Your honor
will excuse me. (*she rises*)

PRINCE OF JINGNAN: Fare you well. (*sees her off*)

PRINCESS: Please do not trouble yourself.

Exeunt PRINCESS, HUAMEI, *and the two* LADIES-IN-
WAITING.

PRINCE OF JINGNAN: Ha, ha . . .

Re-enter SHIYUAN *and* NANNY QIAO.

SHIYUAN: Father . . .

NANNY QIAO: Why is His Lordship so happy? The Princess …

PRINCE OF JINGNAN: (*with a meaningful look at* SHIYUAN) Ha,
ha! Providence! All is providence!

Lights dim.

Epilogue

One year later.

Upstage: XINGYUAN *and* YIXIANG *are seen boating (this may be shown by slides or film). They sing a duet.*

XINGYUAN: Play on with your zither while I warm the wine,

YIXIANG: Congeniality has joined us in marital bliss.

XINGYUAN: Bamboo fence, thatched hut: here our home we'll keep.

YIXIANG: What more to crave in such a life?

XINGYUAN: You care for me and I for you, the world we shall explore,

XINGYUAN AND YIXIANG: (*together*)

And freely roam all lakes and seas and more.

The palace of PRINCE OF JINGNAN, *decorated with lanterns and colored ribbons, is awash with joy. Officials of every rank are on hand to congratulate.*

The marriage ceremony of SHIYUAN *and* PRINCESS YULAN *takes place.*

They freeze.

Lights fade out.

[Chorus, *offstage*]:

> The phoenix's courtship focuses our play;
> With blossoms peach, now blossoms blissful day.
> Who said this is a world of discontent?
> Some flowers for late bloom do have a bent.
> Two kindred spirits love, sincere and just:
> And hand in hand does each the other trust.
> In wintry days with patience let us wait
> Till spring the river-ice does moderate.

Light dims.

The End

臺灣商務印書館 印行

杜思妥也夫斯基 原著
耿濟之 譯

白痴

國家圖書館出版品預行編目資料

背 叛

彭鏡禧・陳芳著.－ 初版.－ 臺北市：臺灣學生，2013.06
面；公分

ISBN 978-957-15-1589-2 (平裝)

854.5   102009306

背 叛

著 作 者：彭 鏡 禧 ・ 陳 芳
著作權所有：彭鏡禧、陳芳 cueariel@gmail.com
出 版 者：臺 灣 學 生 書 局 有 限 公 司
發 行 人：楊 雲 龍
發 行 所：臺 灣 學 生 書 局 有 限 公 司
臺北市和平東路一段七十五巷十一號
郵 政 劃 撥 帳 號 ： 0 0 0 2 4 6 6 8
電 話 ： (0 2) 2 3 9 2 8 1 8 5
傳 眞 ： (0 2) 2 3 9 2 8 1 0 5
E-mail：student.book@msa.hinet.net
http://www.studentbook.com.tw
本 書 局 登
記 證 字 號：行政院新聞局局版北市業字第玖捌壹號
印 刷 所：長 欣 印 刷 企 業 社
新北市中和區永和路三六三巷四二號
電 話 ： (0 2) 2 2 2 6 8 8 5 3

定價：新臺幣二四○元

西 元 二 ○ 一 三 年 六 月 初 版

85403

ISBN 978-957-15-1589-2

不要浪費時間去過別人的生活。不要受制於教條……。
不要讓別人的七嘴八舌淹沒你自己內心的聲音。

前蘋果電腦總裁賈伯斯

2005年在史丹福大學畢業典禮講詞

我們能夠確知的是，莎士比亞經常改寫他人的作品，而
他也預期自己的作品同樣會被人改寫。

史蒂芬‧葛林布萊

當然是文化先書寫我們，我們才書寫自己的故事。

查爾斯‧密

代序：《卡丹紐》計畫

史蒂芬・葛林布萊
哈佛大學講座教授

陳 芳 譯

　　莎士比亞的想像力藉由不停的挪用、改編和變換而運作：他當然有能力自己去創編故事，如《仲夏夜之夢》；但他顯然更喜歡從某些成品中取材，搬移到自己的領域；似乎移動現象本身令他愉悅。他也從未暗示移動必須停止於此：相反的，他好像是故意讓自己的劇作展向無盡變化的可能性。他有一些以多種文本傳世的主要劇作——包含《羅密歐與朱麗葉》、《哈姆雷》、《奧塞羅》、《李爾王》等，或許為了特別的表演方式、演出空間和時間限制，都揭示莎士比亞及其劇團對大量增刪與改變，不以為意。這種自由度，非常直接詳細地顯示這些劇作容許再詮釋、再塑造，促成了莎士比亞偉業的驚人長壽：這些劇作適合變形。

　　不過，問題仍然存在：如何能充分理解戲劇移動？亦即如何充分貼近並置身核心於移動過程中，以便研究、了解這種移動？數年前，我第一次接觸到當代美國劇作家查爾斯・密的傑作時，

覺得至少瞥見了一種可能性。密是一個聰明的回收利用者；對於察覺剽竊材料裡的動人之處，把它轉換到嶄新的、出人意表的方向，他特別有天賦。他的《大愛》令我目為之眩；那是密主要從失傳的希臘戲劇零星、殘存的片段中創作出來的。我對他的很多其他作品也印象十分深刻；他通常把這些作品掛在一個網站上，也不保護版權，以鼓勵他人自由取用，不斷挪用和變造。

　　我聯絡密，告訴他：我希望有機會觀看他的戲劇創作，從最初的發想到實際的製作。我向他解釋，我一直在研究莎士比亞文化材料的創造性移動，但總有 400 年的距離。我想要能夠近距離追蹤和了解每一步進展，而我唯一希望是找到一位活著的劇作家，一位我可以發問並得到直接了當解答的人。我補充說：我已從梅隆基金會得到一筆慷慨的補助，使我為了這項特權，能支付劇作家超乎行情的豐厚酬勞。

　　密婉拒了。他說，他對錢不感興趣，而且特別不喜歡被觀看。但是，他又說，如果我能提出一齣戲的構想，他會考慮和我合寫一些東西。對一個莎士比亞學者而言，選項是相當清楚的：我提議我們合寫一個失傳莎劇《卡丹紐》的現代版。這齣戲是由莎士比亞和他的年輕同事——約翰·弗雷徹合寫的；此人似乎是莎士比亞寫作生涯接近終點時欽點的接班人。他們合作的兩部戲劇——《亨利八世》（《一切都是真的》）與《兩貴親》倖存至今，而《卡丹紐》雖已有好幾種文獻證明曾在 1613 年演出，且在 17 世紀中葉註冊出版，卻不然。它失傳的原因不明，但絲毫不令人意外：16 與 17 世紀的戲劇只有部分保存下來。

　　莎士比亞與弗雷徹顯然是從塞萬提斯《吉訶德先生傳》

（1605）第一部分中插曲式描述的卡丹紐故事取材。當著手創編《卡丹紐》現代版時，查爾斯·密和我從自然合理的時空——卡丹紐的故事開始，可是我們立刻遇到難題：這個故事似乎相對地較難開展。困難不在於安排其背叛和瘋狂的主題。確切地說，乃在於要有一個超強的社會階級為前提——一種遠比財富更具有強制力的東西，才可能展開情節。

密和我可以找到當代有些與文藝復興時期階級社會規範等同的情形——也許在軍隊，或某些極端的商業或學術社群中。但這項工作既不自然又費力，而成功的美學移動靠的是渾然天成，或至少有渾然天成的幻覺。立即點醒我們的東西不是在卡丹紐故事主軸裡，而是在那個故事扭曲的鏡像裡——在塞萬提斯小說中一位神父在旅館朗讀給卡丹紐聽的故事。

神父的故事聚焦於一位名叫安塞摩的年輕人，他莫名地焦慮妻子是否忠貞，使他堅持要自己最好的朋友羅薩柳設法去誘惑她。這個故事不出所料地有悲慘的下場，但我們決定給它一個宜於喜劇的結局。

查爾斯·密和我合寫的《卡丹紐》版本納入一系列典型的莎士比亞母題，於 2008 年在（麻州）劍橋由美國定目劇團（A.R.T.）演出。這齣戲頌讚內心的熱情以及願意為愛冒險。大體的情節，一如莎士比亞喜劇的手法，透過迷亂以臻於淨化與寬恕。

這計畫是一個實驗，使我能研究文化移動實例中，自由與限制的交互作用。而莎士比亞正是這方面的大師。我乃決定額外多作個實驗，以便更深入探討。我聯絡世界各地的劇團，邀請他們

運用相同的材料（現在包括密和我所寫的劇本），再創作一個適合他們獨特文化的演出形式。

　　我很榮幸見證許多改編作品：在印度、日本、土耳其、西班牙、巴西、南非、塞爾維亞、克羅埃西亞、埃及，以及現在——最後也是壓軸的一部——在臺灣。這些文本、製作細節、演出影像已公告在網站上。我所看過的這些作品，非常詳盡地證實了偶然、不羈和限制的混雜，都是我個人文化流動經驗的特徵。沒有一部改編近似另一部，也沒有一部複製我們自己的劇作，即使它們都明顯源自我們所提供的敘事材料；而且，很顯著地，這些作品都是卡丹紐故事的不同版本。集合起來，它們顯示出多種國家劇場傳統的巨大力量。對於人在特定時空中的想像如何受到個別不同歷史所形塑，而之後又如何擷取可擷之物形塑新作，它們提供了有力的線索。

弁　言

　　《背叛》的靈感來自葛林布萊（Stephen Greenblatt）和查爾斯·密（Charles Mee）的美國現代話劇《卡丹紐》（*Cardenio*），後者又改編自「失傳」的莎劇《卡丹紐》；故事源頭則可上溯至西班牙塞萬提斯（Miguel de Cervantes Saavedra, 1547-1616）的著名小說《吉訶德先生傳》（*Don Quijote de la Mancha*）。卡丹紐本來不過是吉訶德旅途中偶遇的人物，卻一變成為跨文化改編的主角。而在「卡丹紐事件」中的插曲，也一變成為廿一世紀葛林布萊與查爾斯·密取材的「原著」。爾後，在梅隆基金會（The Andrew W. Mellon Foundation）的補助下，葛林布萊教授以此劇為本，規畫主持「卡丹紐計畫」（"The *Cardenio* Project"），開始進行「文化流動」（cultural mobility）的劇場實驗（http://www.fas.harvard.edu/~cardenio/index.html）。

　　包含《背叛》在內，至今凡有 12 個不同國家、樣式的「美國版」《卡丹紐》改編演繹本參與了這個計畫。而實驗的基本遊戲規則，就是規定各個作品「背叛」葛林布萊！至於如何背叛，則關乎「在地的」（local）文化思考。也就是說，層層「挪用」的結果，看似步步「背叛」，其實卻可能因此彰顯改編者忠於自我當下文化背景的種種關懷。

　　我們所關心的是：在中國傳統文化制約下，對於「背叛」意涵的中國式和現代化理解。所有與追尋、等待、無悔有關的情感，都應該擁有嘗試的權利，並且得到父權體制某種程度的寬容及諒解。「背叛」，有時只是忠於本心，真的非關背叛，且亦無損於人。在本劇中，主角的背叛行為或可解釋為對家國的忠貞：讓真正有治國理想與能力的人繼承大位，應該更勝於宿命的僵化規定。何況真愛還化解了仇恨，避免了無止盡的冤冤相報。

　　乍看之下，這齣《背叛》與葛林布萊及查爾斯·密的「美國版」《卡丹紐》相距甚遠，似乎是一種背叛，但別忘了他們的版本與「原著」同樣大相逕庭。於是，這種「背叛」，乃成就了另一種「忠實」！至於本劇與《卡丹紐》的唱和、對話，熟稔原著的細心讀者當能體會。

　　感謝葛林布萊教授撥冗作序，梅隆基金會惠予支持，楊世彭教授、劉慧芬主任、李寶春導演提供寶貴意見，周以謙老師慨允將他編寫的曲譜收入本書，陳慧如小姐設計封面。

目　錄

背　叛

彭鏡禧、陳芳

（靈感來自葛林布萊與查爾斯・密劇本《卡丹紐》）

人物表

亦　襄	老人之愛徒，原是朱雀國公主
公　主	玄武國公主毓蘭
行　遠	靖南王世子
世　遠	靖南王次子
靖南王	蒼龍國皇親，功勳彪炳之大將軍
老　人	亦襄之師父，原是朱雀國禁軍統領
喬嬤嬤	靖南王府老奶娘
畫　眉	毓蘭之貼身宮女
柯將軍	靖南王府侍衛長

侍女甲、乙、丙

宮女若干人

侍衛若干人（含甲、乙）

場　目

序　曲

（蒼龍國靖南王府喜氣洋洋，張燈結彩）

（眾侍女忙著布置花廳）

【幕後伴唱】：晴光無限春意動，

　　　　　　　良辰吉日花正紅。

　　　　　　　金玉姻緣三生定，

　　　　　　　關山迢迢千里行。

　　　　　　　玄武宿旗把親送，

　　　　　　　迎風招展入蒼龍。

第一場　拒婚

（靖南王府花廳）

【眾侍女合唱】：迎親──，迎親、迎親、準備迎親，
　　　　　　　　喜事、喜事、喜事臨門。
　　　　　　　　皇親國戚，門當戶對，
　　　　　　　　金枝玉葉，天賜聯姻。（重複）

侍女甲：（抹桌子）……應該早就出發了。

侍女乙：（搬椅子）算算日子，約莫抵達邊界了吧？

侍女丙：（正在掛畫，扭過頭）是啊，聽喬嬤嬤說，這次玄武國
　　　　的送親儀隊很盛大呢！至少也有三、四百人。

侍女甲：聽說玄武皇帝捨不得這個寶貝女兒，不僅指定女宿旗
　　　　隊、虛宿旗隊沿途護送，還派出斗宿旗隊、牛宿旗隊作
　　　　為前導哪。

侍女丙：那咱們蒼龍國豈不是要七宿齊出了嗎？

侍女甲：對啊，角宿旗隊、亢宿旗隊早已抵達邊界，等候迎接花
　　　　轎。氐宿旗隊、房宿旗隊前兩日也已上路。小王爺奉旨
　　　　率心宿旗隊到桑田驛親迎，今日十五，正是啟程的黃道
　　　　吉日喲。

侍女乙：看來皇帝大老爺很疼愛咱們的小王爺嘛。

侍女甲：那當然啦。小王爺相貌堂堂，文武雙全……不疼他要疼
　　　　誰啊？

侍女乙：欸，那你們有沒有聽說，這個玄武國的毓蘭公主長得漂
　　　　不漂亮？溫不溫柔？他們是不是郎才女貌？

侍女丙：（搖搖頭）沒聽說。

侍女甲：（搖搖頭）不知道。

　　　　（喬嬤嬤拄著拐杖上）

喬嬤嬤：你們這幾個傻丫頭！兩國大皇帝結盟賜婚，哪兒管你長
　　　　成什麼樣子！不論是綠豆還是芝麻，門當戶對最重要！
　　　　還不快快打掃，淨在這裡廢話！

　　　　（侍女甲聳聳肩，侍女乙做鬼臉，兩人對看一眼，繼續
　　　　工作）

侍女丙：（迎上）喬嬤嬤！

　　　　（扶著喬坐下，討好地為她搥了兩下背）您老人家歇會
　　　　兒，別著急。您瞧瞧，這可不是都弄妥了嗎？您還有什
　　　　麼不放心的？

喬嬤嬤：（東張西望，指指點點）嗯，嗯，辦這喜慶的事一定要
　　　　處處小心。這牆上的喜幛要是歪一點，那是不吉利……
　　　　窗戶上的囍字若是少一個，就是囍事不到家……這花瓶
　　　　水多了花要謝，水要少了葉兒黃。搬東西輕拿要輕放，
　　　　颱風想著先關窗。還有這裡……哎喲喲喲……你們手腳
　　　　俐落些，還有很多物事要準備啊……

　　　　（侍女甲、乙、丙聽從喬的指揮，開始忙碌起來……邊
　　　　說邊下）

　　　　（黑影幢幢。眾侍衛分批匆忙上場，作尋找狀，邊尋邊

唱）：

找、找、找、四處查找，

尋、尋、尋、仔細覓尋。

哎呀——

突發的事兒，無人能曉，

竟然是啊，良緣變、一似晴天起陰雲；

良緣變、一似晴天起陰雲。

喬嬤嬤：（走上幾步，叫住侍衛長）喂、喂，柯將軍……

　　　　（柯將軍置若罔聞）

喬嬤嬤：我說柯將軍啊……

柯將軍：哦，是喬嬤嬤！

喬嬤嬤：這麼匆匆忙忙、慌慌張張的，在找什麼呀？你們不是該
　　　　出發了嗎？誤了時辰可不得了呀。

柯將軍：（左右看看，壓低音量）唉，我跟您說不打緊，您可別
　　　　說出去啊。

喬嬤嬤：到底是什麼事兒？

柯將軍：心宿旗隊已經等了半晌，辰時早過了，小王爺卻一直不
　　　　見人影啊。

喬嬤嬤：啊？什麼？小王爺不見了？

柯將軍：您小聲點兒！

喬嬤嬤：他去哪兒啦？怎麼沒跟我說一聲？老身可是他的奶娘
　　　　啊！他從小就沒了親娘，都是老身一手帶大的。不管他
　　　　想什麼、做什麼，沒有老身不知道的事兒。他該不會是
　　　　在聚賢堂練劍，忘了時間吧？你們去那兒找找，沒準兒

就找到了……

柯將軍：（打斷她）喬嬤嬤，王府之內俱已找遍。小王爺他——
　　　　好像是離家出走了。

喬嬤嬤：胡說！好端端的，蒼龍、玄武兩國聯姻，他既是靖南王
　　　　世子、蒼龍皇帝的義子，又即將成為玄武國的駙馬，享
　　　　不盡的榮華富貴，幹嘛要離家出走？

柯將軍：可是，小王爺留下書信一封，上面寫得清清楚楚——

（畫外音）

　　……兒固不才，承父祖餘蔭，得祀宗祧；復蒙　皇恩浩
　　蕩，欽賜金玉良緣。位極尊貴，名甚榮顯，不勝僥倖之
　　至。　君父加惠之恩，無以為報，理應殫精竭慮，盡忠
　　孝之義。然自忖人生苦短，歲月飄忽。人生在世，所求
　　為何？不過一知心人耳。兒縱然生性愚魯，亦思有以解
　　惑。是敢冒大不韙，叩請　君父收回成命。……

喬嬤嬤：啊？什麼？這嘰哩呱啦、文謅謅的說了一大串，老身有
　　　　聽沒有懂哪。

柯將軍：唉，喬嬤嬤！（比手畫腳，起【三槍】）如此這般，可
　　　　不是明擺著（小聲）拒婚嗎？

喬嬤嬤：你說什麼？拒婚哦？信在哪裡？老身看看去。

柯將軍：喬嬤嬤，您又不識字，要看什麼啊？

喬嬤嬤：哼！老身雖不識字，可是「鑑定筆跡」的行家！

柯將軍：是、是。王爺方才召見二公子時，還拿在手上呢。

喬嬤嬤：怎麼又要召見二公子了？

柯將軍：唉，小王爺抗旨拒婚，這後果……

喬嬤嬤：那可怎麼辦？

柯將軍：所以，王爺有令，命我急尋小王爺去。現在這個時候，也沒有別的辦法，權宜之計，只能先讓二公子去暫時周旋頂著了。

（看看天色）哎呀！喬嬤嬤，時候不早了，末將還有公務在身，不便久留。告辭了。（匆匆下）

喬嬤嬤：（自言自語）小王爺一聲不響就抗旨拒婚？離家出走？老身才不信！哄我呢？老身看看去。（下）

（切光）

第二場　邂逅

（桃花谷底，外有桃花迷宮）
（表演區Ａ：桃花塢，表演區Ｂ：桃花亭，表演區Ｃ：天然石窟）

（表演區Ａ）
（響起了清幽宛轉的女聲歌唱，伴隨琴音：雨濕蒼苔徑，露冷花木深……）
（行遠躺在石板上，從昏迷中悠悠醒轉。看看周遭，顯得茫然。走到屋外，發現鳥語花香——）
（歌聲持續著：紅顏多不幸，浮生任飄零……）

行　遠：這是什麼地方？我怎麼到了這兒？這歌聲……
　　　　（他循著歌聲走去，卻迷了路）
　　　　怎麼？這小橋、這流水、這湖山石、這芍藥欄、這桃花亭……我該不是在做夢吧？

（行遠步入表演區Ｂ，表演區Ａ燈漸暗）
（表演區Ｂ燈漸亮，亦襄正在撫琴而歌）

亦　襄：（續唱）往事空自省，
　　　　　　　　無奈付東風……

行　遠：（旁白）呀！這是何人……怎生唱來這般淒涼？

　　　　（上前兩步，隔著花叢窺探）

亦　襄：（續唱）一曲《梅花弄》，

　　　　　　　　盡在不言中。

行　遠：（旁白）這位姑娘——

　　　　（旁唱）意態婉約難描畫，

　　　　　　　　人淡如菊薄鉛華。

　　　　　　　　莫非素娥月宮下？

　　　　　　　　容顏更勝海棠花。

　　　　（旁白）這麼年輕貌美的姑娘，怎麼會……？

亦　襄：（驚覺有人）誰在那裡？

行　遠：（走出花叢，拱手為禮）唐突佳人，尚祈恕罪！

亦　襄：（微笑還禮）哦，原來是靖南王世子！

行　遠：（詫異）姑娘是何人？如何認得小王？

亦　襄：此地僻靜，少有外人。昨夜家師攜您回來時，已然交代
　　　　清楚。

行　遠：（回想）昨夜……我只記……得在燈下讀《山海經》，
　　　　……謂大荒之中有合虛山，乃日月之所出……（懷疑）
　　　　啊？我是不是中了迷魂香？

　　　　（亦襄微笑不語）

行　遠：（看看周遭）這是什麼地方？

亦　襄：桃花谷。（略停）家師說，請您來此做客，委屈幾日，
　　　　下月十五，再送您回去。

行　遠：（猛然一驚）今日是？

亦　襄：三月十七。

行　遠：啊！大事不好！小王須得立即趕回。令師是哪位？

亦　襄：師父吩咐不能說。

行　遠：我有急事面見，可否代為通稟？

亦　襄：家師一早即已外出。

行　遠：為何要小王留在此地？

亦　襄：這個嘛，奴家並不清楚。

行　遠：如果小王不願留下呢？

亦　襄：只怕那也由不得您。

行　遠：哈哈！小王自幼習武，祖傳蒼龍劍法。一座小小的桃花
　　　　谷，留不住我吧？

　　　　（略停）恕小王不奉陪了。

　　　　（行遠轉身疾行。亦襄微笑，默不作聲）

　　　　（行遠曲折繞行，遇奇門遁甲之術，以蒼龍劍法回擊。
　　　　煙霧迷漫中，他又回到原處）

行　遠：呀？怎麼又是桃花亭？

　　　　（他嘗試再出走兩次，遇不同變化之奇門遁甲術，最後
　　　　還是回到原處）

行　遠：（看見亦襄仍在微笑）你笑什麼？難道……難道這是一
　　　　座迷宮？

亦　襄：（點點頭）是啊。

行　遠：哈！好一座變幻莫測的桃花迷宮！
　　　　（思索片刻，忽然揮劍刺向亦襄）姑娘，那就麻煩你帶
　　　　路吧。

　　　　（亦裏衣袖一抖，飄出瓣瓣桃花，行遠立即撒劍，頹然
　　　　落坐石椅上）

行　遠：（驚異）啊！這是什麼？為何我忽感全身無力？

亦　裏：噢，這不過是奴家自行研發的「一縷香」。藥效不長，
　　　　兩個時辰罷了。只要不運功，就不礙事。（略停）小王
　　　　爺，既來之，則安之，又何必胡思亂想呢？

　　　　（隨手撥弄兩聲琴弦）

行　遠：唉！好吧。（無奈）小王莽撞，多有得罪。

亦　裏：（嫣然一笑）好說。

　　　　（略停）您大概也餓了吧？請稍待，我去去就來。（下）

行　遠：呀！（唱）這姑娘、舉止神秘、善解人意，

　　　　　　　　彷彿獨立、深谷一幽蘭。

　　　　　　　　她師父、莫測高深、是何主意？

　　　　　　　　倒教我、胡亂想、坐立難安。

　　　　　　　　憂心王府聯姻事，

　　　　　　　　無計脫困把家還。

　　　　（亦裏復上，手持托盤）

亦　裏：小王爺，您趁熱吃了吧。

行　遠：這……（有些遲疑）

亦　裏：放心吧，沒有毒。您是桃花谷的貴客，我們會善盡東道
　　　　之誼。

行　遠：好，多謝姑娘費心！

　　　　（開始大口享用）啊！如此清香，這是什麼？

亦　裏：（微笑）這是我們自己做的桃花餅、桃肉捲，自己釀的

　　　　春桃酒，還有一些桃李乾……

行　遠：好吃！（大口喝酒）好酒！這酒味甘醇，清新自然，是
　　　　如何釀成的？

亦　襄：這酒嘛！（有些得意）可不是用一般的釀造法，而是家
　　　　師自創的加麴蒸餾法。工序十二道，還要以生絹袋盛裝
　　　　細切粉末，九次冷浸在密封的陶瓷罐裡。僅僅材料就有
　　　　十幾樣。這麼瑣碎，像您這種貴人，大概是不會有興趣
　　　　的吧？

行　遠：不（又喝了一口）……呃，姑娘，尚未請教芳名？如何
　　　　稱呼？

亦　襄：我叫亦襄。

行　遠：亦襄姑娘，我在王府從未品嘗過這樣的美酒，（拱手）
　　　　倒要請教。

亦　襄：小王爺啊──

　　　　（唱）粒粒飽滿黃金穗，

　　　　　　　權作酒麴甕底埋。

　　　　　　　鬱金香草浮紫薇，

　　　　　　　炙陽烘培梨果白。

　　　　　　　再借春分桃花蕊，

　　　　　　　細細研磨和杏荄……

行　遠：這很費工哪。

亦　襄：（續唱）穀雨冷泉隔水沸，

　　　　　　　　莫忘琴曲用心栽。

行　遠：哦？還要彈琴給它們聽？如此，要在何處植栽？

亦　襄：（續唱）天然石窟好深邃，
　　　　　　　　洞旁另設一琴臺。

行　遠：（好奇）另設琴臺？小王可以去看看嗎？

亦　襄：（點頭）請！
　　　　（二人起身）
　　　　（續唱）日月精華來點綴，
　　　　　　　　綠意盎然層層排。

（二人繞行步入表演區Ｃ）

亦　襄：（在前引路，邊走邊說）其實每一種植物，都有自己的
　　　　習性，就跟人一樣。比方說吧，桃杏比較偏愛《春曉吟》，
　　　　川芎喜歡《普庵咒》，芍藥愛聽《流水》，桔梗很欣賞
　　　　《廣陵散》……

行　遠：（驚奇）你怎麼知道這麼多？

亦　襄：都是師父教我的啊。

行　遠：咦，你的父母呢？

亦　襄：（眼眶一紅，止步）這……（繼續前行）

行　遠：怎麼了？你為何會來桃花谷？

亦　襄：（搖搖頭）不知道。自我懂事以來，就一直和師父相依
　　　　為命。師父對我很好，但從來不提我的身世，只說我是
　　　　孤兒……（忍淚，拭淚）

行　遠：是我不好，惹得姑娘傷心。

亦　襄：沒有什麼，人各有命。（故作開朗）至少，我還有師父。

（止步）到了，這就是了。

（表演區 C 燈亮）

行　遠：（故意轉移話題）好大一座石窟啊！

亦　襄：是嗎？我們儘量讓這些植物感覺舒適，那麼，它們也會生長得好些。

　　　　（指桃樹）例如這株蜜桃，另外還有個小名，叫做「春蕾」。三月下旬初結果時，為它彈彈《春曉吟》，果實就會特別豐潤；甜美之中，微微帶酸，香氣濃郁，別有風味。

行　遠：慚愧！我只顧著品嘗美食，卻沒想過這些美味是怎麼來的……

　　　　（指著另一株植物）那，這又是什麼？

亦　襄：噢，那是樹莓，須再等上兩個月才會結果呢。把它的果實蒸熟曬乾，可以研磨成粉狀保存。剛才您所食用的桃花餅裡，就加了一點兒樹莓粉。

行　遠：啊，難怪這桃花餅味道獨特，令人齒頰留香啊。

　　　　（環顧周遭）這麼多花草，都是你一人照應的嗎？

亦　襄：以前師父偶爾還會幫忙，這段日子他都沒空，就只有我了。

行　遠：如此說來，真是大不易！

亦　襄：如此說來，天下大不易之事多著呢。

行　遠：你是說……？

亦　襄：我是說——

　　　　（唱）君不見神農藥王嘗百草，

　　　　　　　女媧煉石補蒼天。

　　　　　　　君不見夸父追日到靈寶，

　　　　　　　精衛銜木、欲將滄海填。

行　遠：（續唱）歷歷在目艱與險，

　　　　　　　　事非經過不知難。

亦　襄：（續唱）豈非不知路途險？

　　　　　　　　易與不易一念間。

行　遠：（續唱）隨波逐流

亦　襄：（續唱）非所願，

行　遠：（續唱）但問本心

亦　襄：（續唱）要求全。

行　遠：（續唱）情極無悔

亦　襄：（續唱）亦無怨，

行　遠：（續唱）別有滋味

亦　襄：（續唱）苦作甜。

　　　　（順手照顧花木，白）養花蒔草，釀製酒藥，既是我心
　　　　情願，也就算不得什麼辛苦了啊。

行　遠：（白）姑娘言之成理。對於自己想做的事，是不可能引
　　　　以為苦的。現在左右無事，就讓我來幫你整理這些花圃
　　　　吧。

　　　　（行遠上前協助亦襄，亦襄面露微笑，指點行遠剪枝、
　　　　澆水……兩人狀甚融洽）

【幕後伴唱】：人世間、最難得、惺惺惜惺惺、花草由人戀，
　　　　　　　情投意合、情投意合、浮想也聯翩、也聯翩。

（燈漸暗）

第三場　相知

（靖南王府西廂房）

（畫眉正在門外〔右下舞臺〕和侍女甲、乙、丙閒話）

畫　　眉：你們小王爺，到底是什麼病啊？

侍女甲、乙：（支吾）呃……，是、是……

侍女丙：（搶著回答）是一種很嚴重的病啦！

侍女甲、乙：對、對，很嚴重、很嚴重！

畫　　眉：有多嚴重？

侍女甲：呃……

侍女乙：（同時搶著回答）比瘟疫還嚴重！

**　　丙**：　　　　　　　　是一種失憶症啦！

畫　　眉：啊？到底是什麼？

侍女甲：（勉強解說）是因為瘟疫細菌變種感染所造成的一種失
憶症啦。

侍女乙、丙：（趕忙附和）對、對，真的很嚴重。

侍女甲：（再補上一句）具有很強的傳染力喔！

畫　　眉：（不可置信）失憶症？會傳染？從沒聽說過這種病呀。

侍女乙：這是新品種啦。

侍女丙：只有在我們蒼龍國流行啦，還沒傳到玄武國去……

畫　　眉：啊？什麼？

（喬嬤嬤拄杖上）

喬嬤嬤：你們這幾個傻丫頭，背地裡又在嚼什麼舌根？

　　　　（看到畫眉）哦，是畫眉啊，公主這幾日可好？

畫　眉：托您的福。

侍女丙：喬嬤嬤，我正要去園裡摘花呢。（匆匆下）

侍女甲：大總管要我去東暖閣上取綢緞，我趕時間。（亦匆匆下）

侍女乙：呃，我去瞧瞧針線婆來了沒？（隨下）

喬嬤嬤：（從背後喊著）你們要認真點兒哪，別這麼懶散……

畫　眉：喬嬤嬤，小王爺的病究竟如何？我們公主甚是關心。

喬嬤嬤：他這個病嘛……沒什麼關係，多靜養幾日就好了……

畫　眉：您怎麼知道？

喬嬤嬤：哦，老身剛去看過他。

畫　眉：咦？喬嬤嬤，您怎麼不怕傳染？

喬嬤嬤：傳染什麼？

畫　眉：失憶症呀！

喬嬤嬤：哈哈！老身活了這麼大把年紀，從沒聽說過失憶症會傳染的啊。哈哈！再說小王爺他……（驚覺）誰告訴你他得了失憶症？

畫　眉：聽王府幾位姐妹說，小王爺所患是由瘟疫細菌變種感染所引起的具有強烈傳染力的失憶症（編案：演員要一口氣以誇張語氣很快說完）。您怎麼不怕傳染？

喬嬤嬤：（尷尬）呃，哦……老身每天都跳「有氧舞蹈」，所以具有很好的免疫力啦。

畫　眉：唉，喬嬤嬤，別逗啦。我們都來了好幾日了，一直沒見

到小王爺，也弄不清楚是怎麼回事。洞房沒進，倒進了西廂，簡直兒戲！公主很不高興，今兒一早交代我收拾行裝，看來是打算回國了。

喬嬤嬤：哎喲！那可使不得！

畫　眉：我們公主本是金枝玉葉，受不得半點委屈。她真要任性起來，誰也說不上話呀。好了、好了，我得進去了，東西還沒收好呢。（轉身入房，假裝整理物件）

喬嬤嬤：（旁白）哎呀！這下糟了！小王爺失蹤，至今音訊全無。雖然王爺有令，托言世子染病，暫時搪塞公主。但這也只能瞞得一時啊。如今看來，公主已然起疑。大事不妙！老身得趕緊去稟報王爺。（急下）

畫　眉：（急步到門口目送喬）嘻嘻，待會兒就會真相大白了。

（二宮女上，公主隨上，畫眉迎上攙扶）

【幕後女聲伴唱】：輕移蓮步小嬋娟，

暗香浮動影翩翩。

花樣年華分外豔，

原是國色誇牡丹。

（二宮女立後，畫眉侍立一旁）

（公主讀書，極為專注，不時發出讚嘆聲）

公　主：（唱）連日來如癡如醉神思恍，

辜負了春光明媚百花香。

都只為、這《觀濤集》、金聲玉振非凡響，

一篇篇錦心繡口好文章。

細品味巧思妙手難名狀，

有深意高瞻遠矚濟世方。

不由我含英咀華頻讚賞，

果然是陽春白雪餘音繞梁。

畫　眉：公主，自從您在這西廂房的書櫥裡發現了這卷書，成日
　　　　家就捧著它，早也讀、晚也讀，到底這是卷什麼書啊？

公　主：你們哪裡知道！這一卷詩集文采斑斕，音韻鏗鏘；所論
　　　　博通今古，言近旨遠，真是天下第一才子書啊。

畫　眉：那是何人所作？

公　主：並未署名。（看看書卷）如此文筆，頗有古風，看來不
　　　　是今人之作。本宮倒想認識此人，可惜了……

畫　眉：既然書藏王府，公主不妨問問靖南王，便知由來。

公　主：嗯。

　　　　（公主繼續看書，有時指著書卷與畫眉閒話兩句。畫眉
　　　　間或朝門口張望）

世　遠：（內唱）事有蹊蹺莫能辨，

　　　　（上，續唱）平湖無端起波瀾。

　　　　　　　　兄長離家甚掛念，

　　　　　　　　安撫公主慰家嚴。

　　　　　　　　實情不能露，

　　　　　　　　裝腔解疑難。

畫　眉：（正走到門口張望，噗哧一笑）果然來了！

世　遠：（拱手施禮）畫眉，煩請通稟公主，在下有事求見。

畫　眉：二公子請稍等。

　　　　　（入房）公主，靖南王府二公子求見。

公　主：有請。

　　　　　（畫眉出外，招呼世遠入房）

世　遠：（施禮）參見公主。

公　主：請坐。

世　遠：謝坐。（坐定）

畫　眉：二公子，想必您是來說明世子病情的吧？公主已然等候
　　　　　多時。

世　遠：（非常為難）這個……

公　主：（關懷）怎麼了？是什麼病？

世　遠：是……

畫　眉：是什麼？您倒是快說呀。

公　主：要緊嗎？

世　遠：呃，應該無甚大礙。

公　主：（狐疑）是嗎？二公子莫非有難言之隱？

　　　　　（一揮手，畫眉、宮女均退下）

公　主：如何？

世　遠：（很真誠）在下不敢欺瞞公主，其實家兄——，此時不
　　　　　便說明。總之，請公主稍待數日，家嚴定有交代。

公　主：哦？（凝視世遠，略停）既然如此，本宮暫且不問。

世　遠：多謝公主。（略停）家嚴關心公主長途跋涉，舟車勞頓，
　　　　　這幾日的飲食起居都還習慣否？需要什麼，儘管吩咐下
　　　　　人去辦。

公　主：多蒙垂問，有勞費心。別的倒也罷了，只有一件請教。

世　遠：不敢，還請明言。

公　主：（拿起書卷）二公子可知這卷《觀濤集》是何人所作？

世　遠：（驚訝）啊？公主因何問起？

公　主：本宮偶然得見此書，讀之愛不釋手。作者高才，胸有丘壑，令人不勝傾慕！

世　遠：呀——

　　　　（旁唱）去歲裡閒居時有感世變，

　　　　　　　　藉彩筆抒胸懷寫就詩篇。

　　　　　　　　草編成小卷帙同道賞鑒，

　　　　　　　　誰料想知音人竟在眼前。

　　　　　　　　俏公主殷勤問難掩覥覥，

　　　　　　　　又何妨真心話暢所欲言。

　　　　（白）慚愧！實不相瞞，此乃拙作。

公　主：（驚喜）啊，請恕本宮眼拙，竟不知作者近在眼前。

世　遠：在下輕率成章，貽笑大方了。

公　主：二公子毋須過謙。觀此詩意，作者頗有大志，憂國憂民，躍然於紙。不知緣何而作？

世　遠：公主容稟——

　　　　（唱）去歲終、白虎國、整軍經武，

　　　　　　　屢次挑釁在邊關。

　　　　　　　因逢蘇北大水患，

　　　　　　　皇上不願啟戰端。

　　　　　　　一味忍讓徒示弱，

只怕欺凌難久安。

公　主：（唱）白虎這廝欺人甚，

年初亦來玄武叩關。

父皇年邁未究問，

本宮憂慮在心間。

公子可有治國策？

且來核計道一番。

世　遠：在下以為——

（唱）民為本來君為輕，

固本宜先勸農功。

休養生息減賦稅，

杜絕弊端清政風。

公　主：（續唱）攘外理應先安內，

拔擢賢能濟蒼生。

世　遠：（續唱）五穀新收實倉廩，

輪調黎民去從戎。

公　主：（續唱）民心士氣若可用，

世　遠：（續唱）何愁禦侮不成功？

公　主：（欣喜）著啊！我有同感。

二公子，依你之見，我們該怎麼合作無間，給他們一點

教訓！

世　遠：這倒不難。（手指牆上掛圖）貴國可先屯兵於雁門，再

取道太行；敝國則兵出襄陽，直取咸陽。如此這般，南

北合擊……

（二人開始討論，做各式身段，沙盤推演，相談甚歡）

【幕後伴唱】：萍水有緣初相識，

勝於遠別喜重逢。

一個是神采奕奕言不盡，

一個是溫柔明媚笑語親。

安邦妙計從頭論，

有心人對有心人。

（畫眉上，探頭探腦）

畫　眉：怪哉！這小王爺到底是什麼病啊？公主怎麼一點兒都不
著急呢？

（切光）

第四場　出逃

（桃花谷亦襄房中）

（夜晚，老人與亦襄正在談話）

老　人：……明日午時一刻，（從懷中取出小藥瓶）你將此藥融
　　　　入酒水，讓他服下即可。事關緊要，不可延誤！

亦　襄：師父，這是……啊（訝異），鶴頂紅！這是毒藥呀！為
　　　　什麼……？

老　人：（嚴厲）不必多問！照做就是。

亦　襄：可是，這會奪他性命啊！

老　人：（斬釘截鐵）正是要奪他性命。

亦　襄：師父，您不是說小王爺是桃花谷的上賓，不可怠慢嗎？
　　　　您不是說十五就送他回去嗎？為何現在卻要……？他做
　　　　錯了什麼？

老　人：襄兒，這不是他的錯。只因情勢改變，為師也是情非得
　　　　已。

亦　襄：這些日子，小王爺受困在此，每日挑水澆花、整理草木，
　　　　並無半句怨言……

老　人：那又如何？

亦　襄：師父，難道就別無他法嗎？

老　人：不可因一念之仁而壞了大事。

亦　襄：大事？是何等大事，竟要取他性命？

（老人沉思不語）

亦　襄：師父，（下跪）求求您，放過他吧。您看，桃花谷地形
　　　　險峻，機關布置精巧，反正他也逃不出去，又何必枉殺
　　　　無辜呢？

老　人：他無辜？哼！那是你無知。他身上背負了世世代代的血
　　　　債，打從一出生開始，就有洗不掉的原罪。這原罪嘛，
　　　　（沉思片刻）你是不明白的。

亦　襄：我、我、我下不了手啊。師父，我從來不曾違逆過您，
　　　　但是，殺人……何況是殺一個……一個……

老　人：仇人！

亦　襄：什麼？您說什麼？

老　人：好吧，襄兒，事到如今，或許應該告訴你事實真相。

亦　襄：真相？

老　人：（緩緩點頭）對！真相極為殘酷，這是我保守了多年的
　　　　秘密。

　　　　來，坐下來，聽師父說。

　　　　（老人扶起亦襄，二人坐在石椅上）

老　人：（吟唱）十五年前，蒼龍、玄武兩國聯盟，

　　　　　　　　派大軍突襲朱雀。

　　　　　　　　但見那皇帝、皇后相繼亡，

　　　　　　　　屍橫遍野，猝不及防。

　　　　　　　　奶娘懷抱小公主，

　　　　　　　　精疲力竭、東躲西藏。

　　　　　　　　巧遇老夫在古廟，

臨終托孤將她扶養。

亦　襄：啊——您是說……我就是……

老　人：（點頭）是的，那就是你。後來，老夫就帶著你四處流亡，直到三年前進入桃花谷……

亦　襄：啊，您不僅是我的師父，還是救命恩人啊！

老　人：襄兒，不，公主，事實上老夫曾任先皇禁衛軍統領……當年未能盡忠保護皇室，罪該萬死！老夫是朱雀的罪人啊！

亦　襄：師父！

老　人：這些年來，我一直暗中觀察，總想著有朝一日能報此仇。現在，機會終於來了……

亦　襄：當年的冤仇，跟小王爺有何相關？

老　人：你以為當年統帶聯軍突襲朱雀的大將軍是哪一個？

亦　襄：哪一個？

老　人：就是靖南王！他的爵祿，可是用我們的國仇家恨換來的呀。

亦　襄：天哪！但是，冤有頭、債有主，為什麼不是去殺靖南王呢？

老　人：唉，此中緣由，非你所知。當年聯盟，蒼龍皇帝收下靖南王世子為義子，並與玄武皇帝訂下金玉姻緣，永結百年之好。此時正待大喜，為師的抓走世子，代他留下一封拒婚書信，豈不正好挑起事端，破壞盟約？

亦　襄：啊！師父您……

老　人：這可比毒殺靖南王一人，更能報仇雪恨！
　　　　為師為了盜取世子筆跡，多次冒險潛入靖南王府。現在，

可不能功虧一簣啊！

亦　襄：您已將世子困在桃花谷，現在外面定是鬧得天翻地覆，您的目的亦已達成。何須殺他？

老　人：不，問題就在於：目的……並未達成。不知何故，現在外面……風平浪靜得很。所以，必須殺了他，製造更多事端。

亦　襄：師父，這……

老　人：不必多言。依計而行便是。

亦　襄：我……

老　人：襄兒，切記，這可是不共戴天之仇啊。

　　　　（看看天色）夜深了，不要胡思亂想，快去睡吧！明日還有很多事呢，知道嗎？

亦　襄：師父……

老　人：（拍拍亦襄）好了，去吧！（下）

亦　襄：啊！天啊！我該怎麼辦呢？

【幕後伴唱】：山河破碎人離散，

　　　　　　　失怙之慟年復年。

亦　襄：（唱）師父他一席話、重若千斤擔，

　　　　　　桃花谷頃刻間、不再是世外桃源。

　　　　　　天也旋來地也轉，

　　　　　　還有那陣陣涼意透心寒。

　　　　　　溫言軟語、轉眼成虛幻，

　　　　　　只留下血海深仇苦糾纏。

　　　　　　躊躇不已方寸亂，

漫漫長夜、人不寐、月色無邊。

（徘徊、思索、凝視藥瓶、再思索、再徘徊）

（白）我不能違抗師命……何況這世代冤仇……

【幕後伴唱】：國仇家恨心中怨，

　　　　　　　血債本當用血還。

亦　襄：（轉念，白）但小王爺他……

　　　　（唱）他為人瀟灑磊落寬宏量，

　　　　　　　行止間謙恭有禮不張狂。

　　　　　　　不由我心生情愫暗懷想，

　　　　　　　絹帕之上、錯繡鴛鴦。

　　　　　　　連日他彷彿有言對我講，

　　　　　　　卻總是含情脈脈、話語半掩藏。

　　　　　　　原來那金玉姻緣早定下，

　　　　　　　我只能黯然無語徒自傷。

　　　　　　　縱然是今生盟證無指望，

　　　　　　　也不忍親下毒手、害他一命亡。

　　　　（白）不、不，我不能……（下定決心）也罷！縱使背負不忠不孝的罪名，我也要保全世子！（匆匆下）

【幕後伴唱】：（女）玉漏滴盡天五更，

　　　　　　　　銀河欲曙雨初晴。

（亦襄在前，行遠在後，匆匆上。二人做各式急行身段，包含上坡、下坡、涉溪、躲避各種機關裝置，如金甲武士、十八羅漢等。間或煙霧迷漫，可加爆破特效）

【幕後續唱】：（女）急切切、無心流連觀美景，

　　　　　　　　　意煎煎、匆匆出谷忙趕行。

　　　　　　　（男）顧不得、春寒料峭露濕冷，

　　　　　　　　　顧不得、崇山險峻水又深。

　　　　　　　（女）顧不得、崎嶇斜徑多泥濘，

　　　　　　　（男）顧不得、迷迷濛濛、機關重重、如影隨形。

　　　　　　　（合）戰兢兢、魂甫定，

　　　　　　　　　穿梭花陣、穿梭花陣、步步為營。

　　　（金甲武士陸續出現，圍攻二人。二人舉劍抵擋，做各式劍舞身段。最後，行遠一劍刺向武士，武士倒地）

行　遠：（拉著亦襄）走！

　　　（老人忽上，阻止二人）

老　人：（厲聲）哪裡去？（一劍劈向行遠）看劍！

亦　襄：（衝出，以劍格住）師父！

　　　（轉頭向行遠大喊）快走！

行　遠：（猶豫）亦襄！

老　人：（持續出招）閃開！

亦　襄：（持續阻擋師父的劍招）別管我，快走！

行　遠：保重！（轉身疾步衝下）

　　　（老人欲追）

亦　襄：（棄劍，上前緊緊拉住老人，下跪）師父！

老　人：你、你……（頓足、長嘆）唉！

　　　（切光）

（中卷完）

第五場　捫心

（靖南王府花廳）
（侍女甲、乙正在布置）

侍女甲：（抹桌椅）……原來小王爺是被擄走了！

侍女乙：（貼喜字）想不到竟有這種事！

（侍女丙捧花上）

侍女丙：（整理插花）你們在說什麼哪？

侍女甲：哦，我們正說到小王爺……

侍女乙：不知是什麼人膽大包天，竟敢在太歲爺頭上動土，擅入王府擄人！

侍女甲：王爺應該會追究到底吧？

侍女丙：剛才我聽到王爺下令，交代柯將軍率人去捉拿叛逆呢。

侍女甲：到哪裡捉拿啊？

侍女丙：沒聽清楚，好像是什麼桃花村、李花山的……

侍女乙：幸好小王爺平安回來了。

侍女甲：謝天謝地！

侍女丙：對了，明日世子大婚，喜房裡的貼花都成雙了嗎？

侍女甲：不知道。我在花廳忙了一天，還沒來得及進喜房呢。

侍女乙：我也沒注意啊……

侍女丙：哎呀，那我們趕緊瞧瞧去，免得喬嬤嬤又有得嘮叨了……

（三人同下）

（行遠上）

（投影片：桃花谷中，行遠、亦裏談笑之錄影）

行　遠：（唱）匆匆離谷回王府，

　　　　　　　心中惘然有所失。

　　　　　　　愁眉冷對大喜日，

　　　　　　　難忘顧盼桃花溪。

　　　　　　　並肩入山採茉苡，

　　　　　　　煮酒也曾相偎依。

　　　　　　　恍如一夢憑誰記，

　　　　　　　流光無處覓踪跡。

　　　　　　　隨手寫下相思字，

　　　　　　　始信人間有情癡。

　　　　（白）唉！這君父之命、金玉姻緣，非我所願，委實不妥啊——

　　　　（續唱）幾番思量言又止，

　　　　　　　　怎對父王說端倪？

（靖南王、喬嬤嬤上）

喬嬤嬤：（指指點點）王爺，您瞧，這可不是都準備妥當了嗎？有我盯著，這些丫鬟哪兒敢偷懶啊！這迎春花、爆竹喜、滾繡球，是樣樣不少；米篩籮、炭火盆、合巹酒，是件件俱全啊。

靖南王：好。這禮儀程序一點兒都不能馬虎。

喬嬤嬤：是是是。（看到行遠）唷，是小王爺啊！

　　　　（趕緊行禮）小王爺！

行　遠：（行禮）爹爹！

靖南王：嗯。這些日子難為你了。

行　遠：不敢。（欲言又止）爹爹，這……

喬嬤嬤：小王爺，您莫非是不放心，也要親自巡一遍？哎喲，有
　　　　老身在，安啦安啦！

行　遠：多謝喬嬤嬤。我……

靖南王：嗯？有什麼事？

行　遠：（下定決心）爹爹啊——

　　　　（唱）皇恩浩蕩姻緣賜，

　　　　　　　原是萬幸不敢辭。

　　　　　　　只因歷劫非兒戲，

　　　　　　　歸來輾轉有所思。

　　　　　　　乞請展延婚慶事，

　　　　　　　審慎量度卜大吉。

喬嬤嬤：（旁白）哎喲，嘖嘖嘖，這是什麼說話？

靖南王：（拂袖）哇！胡鬧！

　　　　（唱）異想天開亂綱紀，

　　　　　　　滿口胡言將君欺。

　　　　　　　皇恩浩蕩下聖旨，

　　　　　　　豈容違逆自擇期。

　　　　（白）真是胡鬧！你也不想想這是多大的恩寵啊？這一

　　　　　　聯姻，咱們家世世代代榮華富貴享用不盡哪！

行　遠：爹爹！如此匆忙舉行大婚，想來未必穩當，還是暫緩一
　　　　些時日……

靖南王：住口！你約莫是活得不耐煩了？膽敢跟皇上討價還價？

行　遠：爹爹息怒！小子不敢。只是……

靖南王：只是什麼？既然不敢，就給本王閉嘴！哼！

喬嬤嬤：（頻頻使眼色）呃，我說小王爺啊，您就少說兩句吧。
　　　　且不說聖命難違，王爺為了這婚事，也是煞費苦心啊。
　　　　唔唔唔，就連我們也跟著忙碌了大半年，張羅這個，打
　　　　點那個，誰都沒閒著。這婚事辦得慎重得很哪，一點兒
　　　　也不匆忙。沒準兒您是患了「婚前恐懼症」，才會胡思
　　　　亂想。沒事兒，好好睡上一覺，就好了。

行　遠：這……

喬嬤嬤：（攔住行遠）好了、好了，老身還要陪王爺去巡視喜房，
　　　　忙著呢。
　　　　（招呼王爺下）王爺，這喜房啊，我也交代清楚了……

靖南王：嗯。

喬嬤嬤：喜幛、喜屏、喜枕、喜被……全部雙雙對對，大吉大利，
　　　　包您滿意……
　　　　（王爺看了行遠一眼，隨喬嬤嬤下）

行　遠：（自言自語）這可怎麼好？爹爹這般固執，我總不能跟
　　　　著糊里糊塗吧？
　　　　（思索片刻，決定）也罷！
　　　　（走到桌前，提筆寫信，唱）

富貴榮華何足恃？

不如紅顏一相知。

再次離府留書信，

且問衷心、且問衷心莫遲疑！（下）

（切光）

第六場　情迷

（靖南王府西廂房）

（公主上）

公　主：（唱）半是憂來半是喜，

　　　　　　　心湖陣陣起漣漪。

　　　　　　　莫名緣由何所繫，

　　　　　　　竟然這般不自持。

　　　　　　　欲向花箋訴心事，

　　　　　　　情到深處卻無詩。

　　　　　　　綿綿春雨知我意，

　　　　　　　絲絲不斷任相思、任相思。

（畫眉捧書上，拿給公主。公主接過，看了一眼）

公　主：唉！（隨手置書於桌上）

畫　眉：好容易明日大喜完婚，您怎麼嘆起氣來了？

公　主：嗯，你不會懂的……

畫　眉：難不成是怪王爺籌辦婚事不夠盛大？

公　主：（搖搖頭）不是。

畫　眉：還是怪世子沒來看您？

公　主：（搖搖頭）也不是。

畫　眉：這也不是，那也不是——哦，我知道了，那定是想著……

那個人了……

公　主：不許胡說。

（世遠肩背行囊、長劍上）

世　遠：（唱）徘徊西廂花影裡，

隔葉黃鸝笑我癡。

（畫眉探頭向外看了一眼）

畫　眉：喏喏喏，我不胡說。那個人——來啦。

公　主：哪個人？（起身）

畫　眉：（指指窗外）還有哪個？

公　主：呀！（欣喜）

（畫眉對公主比手畫腳，公主面露嬌羞）

世　遠：（續唱）有情脈脈難啟齒，

最苦今宵別離時。

（世遠行至西廂房門口，畫眉正走到門外）

世　遠：畫眉，煩請通稟。

畫　眉：公主有請。

世　遠：公主怎知我來了？

畫　眉：嘻嘻，心有靈犀嘛。

世　遠：啊？

畫　眉：二公子隨我來啊。

（世遠隨畫眉入房）

世　遠：公主！

公　主：二公子！

　　　　　（向畫眉）奉茶。

畫　眉：是。（下）

公　主：（打量世遠）二公子這身行頭，要做什麼？

世　遠：不瞞公主，在下是來辭行的。

公　主：（一愣）……公子要去哪裡？

世　遠：我已向父王請命鎮守襄陽，以防外患。

公　主：何時啟程？

世　遠：即刻就走。

　　　　　（畫眉持茶盤上，奉茶，侍立一旁）

公　主：為何如此匆忙？

世　遠：這……

【幕後伴唱】：深情從此埋心底，

　　　　　　　話到唇邊意迷離。

　　　　　　　千言萬語非容易，

　　　　　　　各人心事各自知。

世　遠：早晚都是要走的，不如及早。

公　主：公子！

世　遠：（故示歡欣）在下先去整頓軍備，待等公主有令，便可
　　　　　給白虎國來個迎頭痛擊，豈不是好？

公　主：（強顏）如此……也好。

世　遠：在下告辭了。

公　主：公子……好走。

　　　　　（公主目送世遠步出西廂，垂淚掩面下；畫眉隨下）

　　　　　（投影片：世遠、公主在〈相知〉一場相談甚歡之錄影）

【幕後伴唱】：滿懷愁緒無從寄，

　　　　　　　辭別公主兩悲淒。

　　　　　　　無奈姻緣不由己，

　　　　　　　伊人倩影、惟有夢中思、夢中思。

世　遠：（發現地上書信）咦？這是什麼？

　　　　（拾起，展信閱讀）

【畫外音，行遠】：

　　　　「然自忖人生苦短，歲月飄忽。人生在世，所求
　　　　為何？不過一知心人耳。兒縱然生性愚魯，亦思
　　　　有以解惑。是敢冒大不韙，叩請　君父收回成
　　　　命。……」

世　遠：哎呀！難道大哥又被擄走了？這便如何是好？

　　　　（行遠肩背行囊、長劍上，一路尋找東西）

行　遠：（焦急，自言自語）哎呀，到底掉在哪裡啊？怎麼遍尋
　　　　無著哇？

世　遠：（看到行遠，感到奇怪，旁白）呀，幸好不是被擄！這
　　　　是怎麼回事？大哥才剛回來，怎麼又要遠行？

行　遠：（看到世遠）哎呀！不好！（急忙掩藏行囊）

世　遠：大哥要到哪裡去啊？

行　遠：你又要到哪裡去？

世　遠：小弟奉命鎮守襄陽，大哥怎麼忘了？

行　遠：啊，（拍自己腦門）看我這個記性！（尷尬）我……（伸
　　　　手）拿來。

　　　　（世遠交出書信，行遠接過，收好）

世　遠：大哥，明日可是您和毓蘭公主的大喜啊，您這是……？

行　遠：二弟……唉！既然被你撞見，我索性就對你實說了吧。
　　　　愚兄是不可能和公主成親的……

世　遠：（大驚）啊？卻是為何？

行　遠：因為……因為我已另有意中人了。（欲行）

世　遠：大哥不可。（伸手阻攔）皇上有旨，您一定要娶公主。

行　遠：讓開！

世　遠：不。您這麼一走了之，如何對公主交代？

行　遠：（格開）愚兄顧不了那麼許多。

世　遠：（擋住）您不能不顧公主！

行　遠：閃開！不然我就要出手了。

世　遠：不！您一定要與公主完婚。

行　遠：好！就來看看你能否攔得住我？

　　　　（二人各出劍招，你來我往，非常激烈。行遠兩度可以
　　　　抽身，都被世遠奮不顧身撲上。忽然，行遠躍開兩步）

行　遠：慢著！明日是我的大喜，你怎麼選在這個時候趕去襄
　　　　陽？

世　遠：我……唉，大哥，我也索性對您實說了——
　　　　（唱）世子失蹤闔府亂，
　　　　　　　奉命西廂兩周旋。
　　　　　　　錯愛公主自縛繭，

　　　　　　決意出走了情緣。

行　遠：（驚訝）呀！（轉念一想，微笑）原來如此。愚兄倒有
　　　　個主意，可以兩全其美。

世　遠：此話怎講？

行　遠：二弟啊——

　　　　（唱）我本疏懶性散淡，
　　　　　　　不拘俗禮好林泉。
　　　　　　　身為世子須檢點，
　　　　　　　鐘鼎枷鎖苦難言。

世　遠：（續唱）大哥何以出此言？
　　　　　　　　　皇上有旨賜良緣。
　　　　　　　　　悔約背盟恐結怨，
　　　　　　　　　辜負公主心怎安？

行　遠：（續唱）桃花谷中尋真愛，
　　　　　　　　　世子之位你承擔。
　　　　　　　　　締結駕盟定良策，
　　　　　　　　　一展長才天下安。

世　遠：（續唱）小弟不敢生妄念，
　　　　　　　　　丹心一片可問天。

行　遠：（續唱）蒼天有意早盤算，
　　　　　　　　　宛轉指引把花攀。

世　遠：這……
　　　　（續唱）不知伊人可情願？
　　　　　　　　　還須商量圖周全。

行　遠：（續唱）事不宜遲當機斷，

　　　　　　　勸二弟、面見公主佳話傳。

世　遠：大哥，我才剛去向公主辭行啊。

行　遠：這有何妨？再去一回，換套說辭便是。

　　　　二弟，父王已派人前往桃花谷，愚兄須立即趕去。（微
　　　　笑，取出書信）此信原要順道留在書齋，現在就煩你代
　　　　為轉呈父王了吧。

世　遠：（接過書信）大哥……

行　遠：（凝視世遠）後會有期。

世　遠：（凝視行遠）大哥保重。

行　遠：保重。

　　　　（二人作別，分下）

　　　　（切光）

第七場　無悔

（桃花谷底）
（柯將軍與眾侍衛急上）

柯將軍：（【急急風】）眾將官，急攻桃花谷！王爺有令，務必
　　　　生擒活口！

眾侍衛：遵命。

　　　　（煙霧迷漫，金甲武士等機關裝置不時出擊，與柯將軍
　　　　等人交戰。老人、亦襄上，交戰中敗下）

老　人：（左右張望）老夫早知會有今日，已備下小船……來，
　　　　我們上船去。小心！
　　　　（柯等趕上攔阻）

柯將軍：想逃？沒有這麼容易！（揮劍砍去）

亦　襄：（驚叫）師父！

老　人：（格住，回刺）哈哈，就憑你們這幾個，也想攔住老
　　　　夫？

柯將軍：那就試試！
　　　　（眾人圍攻老人，亦襄欲揮袖）

柯將軍：（抓住亦襄）姑娘老實點兒！不要亂施迷藥！

亦　襄：啊！

老　人：（阻擋劍招，擔心）襄兒，沒事吧？

柯將軍：老頭兒，你乖乖束手就擒，這位姑娘就沒事。不然……

老　人：你想怎麼樣？

柯將軍：不怎麼樣，只不過——把她大卸八塊。

老　人：你敢！（衝過去，劍劈柯）

柯將軍：（把亦襄推給其他侍衛）綁起來！（侍衛綁住亦襄）

　　　　　（柯與老人拆招幾回合）

　　　　　咦？這是……朱雀劍法？

老　人：哈哈，好眼力！

柯將軍：你是何人？

老　人：不必多問！接招！（快攻）

柯將軍：慢著！（躍開一步）這兩招——「孔雀開屏」、「雀屏
　　　　　中選」，獨傳皇室宗親，你到底是何人？

老　人：哼！廢話少說！（搶攻）

柯將軍：大家一起上！絕不能讓他逃走！

　　　　　（眾人圍攻，老人漸漸不支。柯一劍刺中老人右臂）

老　人：（棄劍，左手搗住傷口）啊！

　　　　　（眾侍衛團團圍住，劍指老人）

老　人：（頹然）唉！上天亡我，其如命何！

　　　　　（左手忽奪一侍衛劍，欲自刎）

　　　　　（行遠躍上，以劍挑開）

行　遠：且慢！（劍轉一圈，逼退眾侍衛）

眾侍衛：（躬身行禮）小王爺！

行　遠：柯將軍，爹爹有令，這裡由我處理。我命令你們即刻退

出桃花谷！

柯將軍：（與眾人面面相覷）這……

行　遠：怎麼？你們膽敢違令？

柯將軍：末將不敢。只是王爺先前吩咐，務必擒拿谷中叛逆，帶回王府審問。剛才末將發現，（指著老人）此人疑似朱雀餘孽……事關重大，所以……

行　遠：哦？是嗎？（看看老人，又看看亦裏）休得胡說！朱雀早已滅絕，你有何憑證？

柯將軍：回稟小王爺，他所使的劍招，是朱雀皇室獨傳之秘，外人絕不可能得知。

行　遠：是嗎？祖傳武功秘笈外流，亦屬平常。先不要胡亂猜測。

　　　　　柯將軍，借一步說話。

　　　　　（行遠與柯向前兩步，低聲）其實，爹爹另有任務交代於我，此時不便明言。你們先撤回去吧。

柯將軍：是，末將遵命。（手一揮，率眾侍衛下）

　　　　　（行遠急趨前為亦裏鬆綁）

行　遠：我來遲了，你們沒有受傷吧？

亦　裏：多謝相救。師父手臂有傷。

行　遠：（關心）傷得如何？

老　人：哼！用不著你來貓哭耗子！要不是你，這些侍衛怎麼會來？他們怎麼進得了桃花谷？

行　遠：前輩請息怒。這確是晚輩的不是。但我一得知家嚴派出高手，就日夜兼程趕來，唯恐這裡有什麼閃失……

亦　襄：小王爺，你為何回來？

老　人：難道不怕老夫殺你嗎？還是回去準備你的親事吧！

行　遠：這……晚輩不敢欺瞞。我已放棄世子之位，再也不回去了。

老　人：（驚訝）什麼？

亦　襄：（驚訝）這是為何？

行　遠：（嚴肅）亦襄，自我回到王府——

　　　　（唱）紅燭下、夜夜無眠聽鐘漏，

　　　　　　　綺窗前、獨對天邊月如鉤。

　　　　　　　恍惚間、耳畔常聞《菩庵咒》，

　　　　　　　卿卿啊、一顰一笑浮心頭。

　　　　　　　魂夢縈、方知傾心由來久，

　　　　　　　世子名、金玉緣、到此兩拋丟。

　　　　　　　且留書、表明心跡君父奏，

　　　　　　　惟願取、天長地久、攜手泛輕舟。

　　　　（向老人下跪，白）請您成全。

亦　襄：（感動）你……（轉向老人，亦下跪）師父——

　　　　（唱）世事荒唐多誤謬，

　　　　　　　冤冤相報幾時休？

　　　　　　　機關算盡苦追究，

　　　　　　　得不償失豈良謀？

行　遠：（續唱）漁樵閒話千載後，

　　　　　　　依然白雲去悠悠。

亦　襄：（白）師父，求求您——

亦、行：（合唱）冤家宜解不宜結，

　　　　　　　　凤昔仇怨一筆勾。

老　人：（看看行遠，再看看亦襄，對行遠）你剛才所說的，都
　　　　是真的嗎？

行　遠：晚輩對天發誓，絕無半句虛假。

老　人：你不後悔拋棄名利、背叛家國嗎？你不擔心背負不忠不
　　　　孝的罪名嗎？你能甘於粗衣蔬食的生活嗎？

行　遠：（看著亦襄）亦襄曾經說過：只要是我心情願，再怎麼
　　　　辛苦，都算不得什麼。（向老人）前輩，我確實是心甘
　　　　情願的啊。

老　人：天意啊！（仰頭看天）一切都是天意！罷了！
　　　　（對行遠）世子，行遠，你要好好照顧襄兒，不然，老
　　　　夫絕對饒不了你。

行　遠：前輩放心！

亦　襄：多謝師父！

老　人：你們都起來吧。

　　　　（行遠攙扶亦襄，二人起立）

行　遠：前輩，方才我不過是虛與委蛇，暫時哄得他們離去。不
　　　　消幾時，他們必會折返。桃花谷是不能再逗留了……

老　人：毋須擔心。來，老夫已有準備。

　　　　（三人互相扶持，上船。行遠解纜，划船前行）

【幕後伴唱】：青山嫵媚雲出岫，

　　　　　　　垂柳拂岸景致幽。

　　　　　　　桃花含笑頻回首，

　　　　從此風月不知愁，不知愁。

（船漸下）

（切光）

第八場　拒婚

（深夜，靖南王府花廳）

（靖南王震怒中）

靖南王：（手持書信）……荒唐！荒唐！真是不忠不孝！這分明是背叛！背叛君父，目無家國，他就這麼一走了之，要本王如何向皇上和玄武國交代？

世　遠：爹爹請息怒。大哥臨行前已然囑咐……

靖南王：（怒責世遠）你也忒不像話！不但不攔住他，還幫襯他！現在可好，明日大婚，文武百官齊集一堂，新郎卻不見人影，為父顏面何在？

世　遠：爹爹，毓蘭公主她……

靖南王：對，公主！本王要如何向公主解釋？這次還能有什麼理由？還能再拿生病作藉口嗎？公主再明理，也不會縱容這樣的駙馬！哼，這個逆子啊！放著好好的世子不做，丟下現成的富貴，他到底是中了什麼邪？

世　遠：爹爹，大哥這麼做，也是出於無奈，他……

靖南王：住口！「國有國法，家有家規」，豈能容他這般恣意妄為？

來人哪！

（侍衛甲上）

侍衛甲：在。

靖南王：快馬前去桃花谷，傳本王口諭，讓柯將軍把這個逆子一
　　　　起抓回來見我！

侍衛甲：是。（下）

　　　　（喬嬤嬤上，險些撞到侍衛甲）

喬嬤嬤：哎喲！怎麼回事啊？慌慌張張的……

　　　　（看看王爺，再看看世遠）王爺，幹嘛生這麼大的氣呀？

靖南王：哼！喬嬤嬤，你自己看看！（遞信給喬）

喬嬤嬤：（接過來正著看、再倒著看）哎喲，王爺，您忘了，老
　　　　身不識字啊。

　　　　（再仔細看）不過，這好像是行遠的筆跡嘛。（再顛倒
　　　　看）怎麼看來跟上回一模一樣啊？哎喲！不好了！又有
　　　　一封假信，（緊張）世子又被擄走了！難怪老身今兒個
　　　　一整天都不對勁兒……

世　遠：喬嬤嬤，這封信倒是不假，大哥這回是真的出走了……

喬嬤嬤：什麼？他去哪兒了？怎麼沒跟我說一聲？

靖南王：哼！這逆子連本王都未曾稟報……

喬嬤嬤：（忽然想起）哎呀！明日的大婚怎麼辦哪？

世　遠：公主她……

　　　　（侍衛乙上）

侍衛乙：啟稟王爺，毓蘭公主駕到。（下）

靖南王：呀！這……（攤手）你們都先迴避吧。

眾　人：是。

　　　　（眾人下。王爺急忙出迎，二宮女、公主、畫眉上）

靖南王：（緊張）不知公主深夜駕臨，有失遠迎，尚祈恕罪。

公　主：王爺不必多禮。（坐定）請坐。

靖南王：謝坐。（坐定）

公　主：王爺可知本宮到此為了何事？

靖南王：（忐忑）這……這卻不知。

公　主：本宮奉旨南來，這一路之上，留心風土人情。貴國擁有
　　　　良田萬頃，物產豐饒，民風亦淳樸可愛；敝國卻是牛羊
　　　　群集，人民習於狩獵攻戰。而今白虎國屢屢生事，蒼龍、
　　　　玄武合則兩利，可以互補有無，同聲連氣。王爺想必是
　　　　明白的吧？

靖南王：（一時不知如何回應）是、是，公主所言甚是。

公　主：正因如此，你我兩國結盟，事關重大。

靖南王：是、是。

公　主：如果結盟不成，後果——可是不堪設想的。

靖南王：（惶恐）還請公主明示。

公　主：本宮以為，這結盟嘛，是一回事；聯姻，則是另一回事。

靖南王：啊？

公　主：王爺——

　　　　（唱）父母之命媒妁言，

　　　　　　　聽天由命實堪憐。

　　　　　　　既是終生知心伴，

　　　　　　　何妨尋覓夙世緣。

靖南王：公主的意思是……？

公　主：自從盤古開天闢地以來，咱們女兒家總是不能自主，事
　　　　事都要聽命於君父。然而——

　　　　　　（續唱）自作主張自揀選，

　　　　　　　　　　寧為玉碎莫瓦全。

　　　　　　　　　　任憑流年暗中換，

　　　　　　　　　　好花終開並蒂蓮。

靖南王：（支吾）呃……

公　主：（語氣平穩）本宮與世子素不相識，如今又緣慳一面。
　　　　既然好事多磨，也就不必勉強。本宮決定修書稟陳　父
　　　　皇，三日後啟程北返。

靖南王：啊？那……那明日……明日……

公　主：明日嘛（似笑非笑）──自然無事。（略停）想必您可
　　　　以妥善處理才是。

靖南王：這……這……

公　主：王爺，本宮還有一言。

靖南王：公主請說。

公　主：二公子雄才大略，博學多聞，實為不世出之人才。

靖南王：（意外）哦？世遠？

公　主：本宮有意，相煩二公子隨行，至敝國共商防禦大計。不
　　　　知王爺能否俯允？

靖南王：啊？（恍然）哦，是、是，這個自然，這個自然。犬子
　　　　理應護送公主，多謝公主不棄。

公　主：（微笑）王爺，相信蒼龍、玄武兩國，必能同心協力，
　　　　邦誼永固。

靖南王：是，多謝公主。

　　　　（打三更鼓：咚！──咚！咚！）

公　主：已交三更，不多叨擾，本宮告辭了。（起身）

靖南王：公主慢走。（相送）

公　主：留步。

　　　　（公主、畫眉、二宮女下）

靖南王：哈哈……

　　　　（世遠、喬嬤嬤上）

世　遠：爹爹……

喬嬤嬤：王爺怎麼這麼高興啊？公主她……？

靖南王：（意味深長看著世遠）哈哈，天意啊！一切都是天意！

　　　　（切光）

尾　聲

（一年後）

（上舞臺，行遠、亦襄行船而過〔此段或可以投影顯現〕）

行　遠：（唱）卿撫琴絃我煮酒，

亦　襄：（續唱）宛轉同心結綢繆。

行　遠：（續唱）竹籬茅舍共相守，

亦　襄：（續唱）人生到此復何求？

行　遠：（續唱）相知相惜天涯走，

行、亦：（合唱）五湖四海任遨遊。

（靖南王府喜氣洋洋，張燈結彩，文武百官前來賀喜）

（世遠迎娶公主，拜堂完婚，定格，燈轉弱）

【幕後伴唱】：鸞鳳求凰譜新曲，

　　　　　　桃之夭夭待佳期。

　　　　　　休道世事不如意，

　　　　　　花開也有恁般遲。

　　　　　　但將真情酬知己，

　　　　　　執子之手莫相疑。

　　　　　　且耐餘寒未盡日，

　　　　　　春江終有水暖時。

（切光）

精選曲譜
Selected Scores

周以謙 作

樂譜繕打 周以謙

君不見
Haven't you heard

Andante

君不見—— 神農

藥_王嘗_百_草 女媧煉石補蒼_天——

君不_見 夸父追_日 到_靈寶——

精衛銜木 欲將蒼海填—— 歷歷在目 艱與險 事非

經_過 不知_難—— 豈非不知 路途險 易與

不——易 一念—間——

隨波逐——流 非所—願 但問本心 要_求—

全　情極無悔亦無怨　別有滋味　苦＿作＿＿＿＿＿甜

去 歲 終
At last year's end

去＿歲＿終　白虎＿國整軍＿經

武屢＿次挑＿釁＿在＿邊＿關　因逢蘇＿北

大＿水＿患皇上不願啟戰＿端　一＿味忍＿讓

徒示弱＿＿＿＿只＿怕欺＿凌＿難久＿安白＿＿

虎這＿廝欺人甚年＿初亦來玄武＿＿叩

關父＿皇年邁未究問本宮憂慮在心＿＿＿＿＿

間公子可有治國策　且＿來核＿＿＿計＿＿＿

·背叛·

道 一 番

民為本來君為輕 固 本宜 先 勸 農 功

休 養生息 減 賦 稅 杜 絕 弊 端

清 政 風 攘 外 理 應先 安 內 拔

擢 賢 能 濟 蒼 生 五 穀 新 收 實

倉 廩 輪 調 黎 民 去 從 戎 民心 士氣 若 可用

何 愁 禦 侮 不 成 功

· 64 ·

玉漏滴盡
The sandglass shows

穿梭花——陣——步_步為——營

匆匆離谷
In haste I left the Valley

Largo

匆——匆——離——谷

回——王 府　　心——中 惘——然 有——所

失　　　愁 眉——冷——對 大——喜——日

難 忘——顧——　　盼——　　　　桃 花——

溪　　　並——肩 入——山 採 茱——茳——

煮 酒——也——曾 相——偎——依　　恍 如

一一夢 憑誰　　記 流　光　無　處

覓蹤　　　跡 隨手　寫　下 相思　

字 始信　人　間 有　情　癡 幾番

思量言又 止怎對　父　王 說端　　倪

One half worry

Largo

鸞鳳求凰

The phoenix's courtship